A True Gift

a collection of short stories and poems

Sean Lovedale

WESTBOW·
PRESS
A DIVISION OF THOMAS NELSON
& ZONDERVAN

WestBow Press books may be ordered through booksellers or by contacting:

WestBow Press
A Division of Thomas Nelson & Zondervan
1663 Liberty Drive
Bloomington, IN 47403
www.westbowpress.com
1 (866) 928-1240

Remember, the story is in the telling of the story and these stories are fiction.

ISBN: 978-1-4908-5269-0 (sc)
ISBN: 978-1-4908-5270-6 (hc)
ISBN: 978-1-4908-5268-3 (e)

Library of Congress Control Number: 2014918274

Printed in the United States of America.

WestBow Press rev. date: 01/14/2015

Thanks to my Father God, family and friends who
without I would have no stories to tell.

Compassion and gratefulness are our greatest
possessions, whether we are rich or poor.

Contents

1

I'm a Farmer

"You see that, Jerome? There goes Joe in that stretched-out Cadillac. I don't believe I ever saw him but a few times in anything but his old Ford pickup truck." I reflected on that fact. *The year of Joe's truck changed over the years, and Joe never bought a new truck, but he always bought a Ford.*

Joe and I had run into each other years ago, on Main Street in our little town, when he had just driven into town in a '56 Ford 150. "This bucket of rust got me across four states without as much as one misfire," Joe had told me as he patted its fender. Our friendship had begun on that day when I paused to look at his rough-looking truck.

"Now they have him in the back of the Cadillac," I said to my nephew Jerome. "It doesn't seem right."

I had come up to the crossroads to watch my friend go by—I didn't want to, but I did. My nephew sat next to the passenger window in what I am sure some people would consider just an old Chevy truck. There were dents from getting too close to a tree or two, or misjudging the distance of farm equipment, and there were a couple of good caved-in places in the pickup's body where my old bull tried to duel with me and my truck. My pickup truck probably didn't have a straight section on the body and had only been washed by God when He let it rain.

The doctors tell me that my nephew, who helped me on the farm, has Down syndrome—people say it like that is supposed to be bad. Yet Jerome listened, and when Jerome said something, the wisdom in his

1

voice usually shook me to the bones. It was like he knew things—things only God knew. Or maybe it was like Jerome had an eye into heaven. I loved having him with me. He didn't irritate me like other folks did with their superficial thoughts and their worries about this futile thing or that.

I watched as all the cars, with their headlights turned on, followed the Cadillac with my friend Joe laid out in the back. I am glad they were there because I couldn't be.

Joe was the one I talked to when I found out that Josefina had another man, and she thought he was a better man than me. Joe was the one who quietly kept me company when my mother died and I couldn't understand life without her. Joe was the one held me up when my grandson didn't come back from Iraq. There will be those who wonder why I wasn't at the church or at the graveside, but I was there when his firstborn died in the Corvette that Joe bought him, and Joe sobbed—there was no place else to be but sitting out in that pasture with a bottle of Crown and a milk jug of warm water. We passed each bottle back and forth until all the emotion had run out on that prairie grass.

Jerome pulled me out of my memories when he said, "He likes Fords. What was wrong with his flatbed Ford? The one he used to feed his cows. Joe would have fit on it."

"I think you are right because that shiny hearse doesn't cut out right, and I never saw him wash any vehicle other than the car he used to drive Mary to church."

"Why did they do that?" Jerome looked at me with the big straightforward eyes he always had.

"I don't know, and they probably put Joe in a suit—I never saw him in anything but his bib overalls, even when he was on his way to the Methodist church with Mary, who was always dressed real nice." I just watched and then said, "We are the same; we are farmers."

A few raindrops spattered on the windshield as we watched Joe's procession. I couldn't help but smile, "Looks like the rain is here— thank you, Jesus. We need the rain, and I love the rain, the way it makes everything fresh and green."

Jerome smiled. "Joe's in heaven in his bib overalls, and he's smiling."

***

Jerome helped me when I found an old '70 Chevy one-ton truck sitting out in the weeds, a couple of hours away in Nebraska. The man told me that the engine had a hole in the side of the block and that there was some rust in the cab, but that the truck's four-speed transmission and all else seemed to be just fine. I gave him five hundred dollars, and he gave me a signed title. I looked at the title and realized that he bought the truck when it was a year old. He had had that truck a long time. I watched him in the rear view mirror as he watched Jerome and me pull away. He just stood there until we were out of sight—he was a farmer like me.

Jerome and I got the truck home, and soon we had the engine sitting on the floor, with the other parts, which had to be removed in order to remove the engine, laying on benches and tables in the barn—it's where we used to stack hay until the big round bales became the way to put up hay. I had a 327 on an engine stand that had come out of a '67 Chevy Impala. Jerome and I looked it over and decided that all we had to do was change out the water pump, from a short nose to a long, and all would work. We did so, as we had thought, and Jerome had a smile that I equate with an angel's smile—all the angels in the Bible were males, and Jerome could have been one, as far as I was concerned—when I turned the ignition switch and the desired rumble flowed out of the single exhaust.

From there on out, Jerome and I worked. We repaired every little thing. We started with checking the brake bands, brake cylinders, and all that made the truck stop. We made sure that the drive line was perfect and had to replace the U-joints. Everything that required fluid or grease got new. All the light bulbs were replaced, and we made sure that all the electrical connections were making good contact with silicone dielectric grease. I never had a better time than when Jerome and I were perfecting this truck.

We did wash it after we got some mud on it because we had worked hard at getting all the dents out and painting it back to its original color. Neither one of us knew how to do body work, but modern times brought us to YouTube, and I typed in the words as my son, who was no longer with me, had taught me, and we found videos that showed us how to get

3

the body of this old truck straight. It was interesting how Jerome and I would sit next to each other, and he would pull something different out of the video than I did.

The boy had wisdom that if people would stop and listen, they might hear something different from what they expected. Maybe his speech wasn't perfect, and he didn't care about fashion or whether he had a haircut, but the young man had wisdom. Between the two of us, we made the truck as perfect as I could ever see it happening.

***

Jerome said, "That's my uncle, and I remember. You take him to the cemetery in the truck that he and I built." He looked at the quiet mortician and the family gathered in the room. "Well, that's what he wanted," Jerome pleaded.

The mortician reasserted that the proper way to take a "loved one" to the cemetery was in his hearse, and he assured everyone that it was a top-of-the-line automobile. Everyone was quiet and okay with the hearse—except Jerome.

"But that is a Cadillac, and my uncle said he had never ridden in a Cadillac and never would," Jerome argued. "He told me that all he ever drove was farm trucks, and he wanted the Chevy that he and I built to be used when it was his time to go to the graveyard."

"Now, Jerome, I know you may not understand, but that has a flatbed on the back, and my brother might slide off." Jerome's aunt had her hand on his knee and looked at him with pitiful eyes.

Jerome pulled his leg back. "You never listen to me, but my uncle did, and I listened to him, and he wants to go in his truck because ... he's a farmer." Jerome wouldn't give in. "Besides, we put tie-down rings on the flatbed, and my uncle has some straps." Jerome was satisfied with the solution.

The argument continued between Jerome and the others who thought that they had a say in this old farmer's funeral. It continued until the mortician looked as if he would rather be someplace else. The alarmed mortician's secretary was right behind Mr. Denmark when he burst into the room, saying, "I have been reading my friend's will, and part of his will pertains to his funeral." There was silence in the room because in this small town, Mr. Denmark was a respected lawyer. Mr. Denmark was rarely seen outside his office and always held a presence that was noticed when he was around. "His will states that he won't be buried in a suit but in his own bib overalls—not new ones."

Jerome beamed. "I have the overalls he liked the best here," he said and held up his plastic grocery sack. "My uncle told me, and I listened."

"One more thing—it seems that this man you are about to bury doesn't like Cadillacs but wanted to take his last ride on the back of his '70 Chevy flatbed. Not only that, but Jerome is to drive the truck."

"But Jerome doesn't have a driver's license," Jerome's always-vocal aunt interjected.

"My uncle has been teaching me, and I can drive," Jerome insisted. "I only want to drive this one time. My uncle was my friend—he listened to me." Jerome, who was always quiet when most people were around, was to be heard.

"This is a bunch of bull!" The sister of the deceased took over the discussion, "My brother has never been to a funeral, and those things he wrote don't make any sense. I bought a good suit for him, and I like that hearse—it is best." Then silence fell on the room.

After the long silence, the mortician, who had been fiddling with some papers, spoke up. "There are some things you folks most likely don't know," he said, and he looked over the group that took up every chair in his meeting room. "You most likely think that this man you call brother, uncle, and friend was not a religious man because he never attended church, he was never at a funeral service, and he was never at a graveside—and I know that because I am in these places. But what you don't know is that he showed up at my funeral home every evening before anyone in this little town was to be buried. He knelt and prayed at their coffins, he asked our God to accept them into His kingdom and for their family's well-being and salvation. Plus, it didn't make any difference to him how the person in that coffin was viewed by the people of this town; he was here the evening before. There were three people that no one paid a dime for their interment. There was no one to attend a funeral if there had been one, and no one was at their gravesides when they were put in the ground, but this man you claim you know paid for their coffins and expenses and prayed at their coffins."

"My brother didn't pray and wouldn't even talk about God. I do not believe you," this sister said, from under her perfect hair and above her perfect dress.

"Your brother never talked about these things. Yet after a while, I expected him the night before every funeral, and I watched as he pulled his small Bible out of the pocket of his overalls and prayed.

"That was the one he read to me from," Jerome said, happy to have an ally. Jerome turned to his aunt. "You would never listen to him. You only talked to my uncle."

The sister and aunt paused for a moment.

"I've talked to the sheriff," the lawyer cut in, "and he won't say a word when Jerome drives the truck to the cemetery. His men will be there to make sure, as they always do, that your procession won't be interfered with, but they won't bother Jerome." Jerome beamed.

"My brother didn't have a Bible, and I don't know what you are talking about." This sister of the deceased forced her thought out onto all who would listen, and all eyes were on the Bible she held on her knees, which appeared as if it had never been opened, with its undisturbed ribbon in the middle of the book.

"Well, you remember that I was the one who was asked to pick up my friend when he passed. I have to admit that this was a hard one to go to, and I have seen a lot of people at the end of their lives." The mortician looked at his desk. "This is what I took for myself because I wanted to know what drove this man—this man to whom I rarely talked and called friend in my heart; maybe I shouldn't have." The mortician held out a small worn Bible, with rubber bands holding the pages in.

The sister leaned forward in her chair. "That is not my brother's Bible. He didn't believe, and he never had a Bible."

Jerome appeared to be dancing in his chair at the sight of the worn book. "He read to me out of that one, and his name is in it,"

"No, I don't believe it." The sister was sure.

6

The mortician saw that Jerome looked both sad and happy at the sight of the old Bible and said, "As I have said, I shouldn't have taken the Bible. Jerome, would you like to have it?"

Jerome didn't hesitate and had his uncle's Bible instantly held to his chest. Jerome looked downward, and the mortician couldn't decide if he was comforted or praying, but then he thought maybe it was both.

***

The day came for the church ceremony, and some commented on the oddness of my lying there in my bib overalls. I watched from my advantage point, as Jerome had made sure my casket was strapped down good, just like I had taught him to check any load we were hauling. Then he opened the door to the cab of my truck and rain splattered on my coffin. Jerome smiled and said, "There's your rain, Uncle—just like you like it." Then Jerome drove me to the resting place of my earthly body.

They had a little get-together at the café on Main Street, not far from where Joe and I met, after all the doings about my leaving them. I was glad for my family and friends getting together in the small café. It was the place where I drank my morning coffee sometimes and made jokes or talked about the abundance or lack of rain with my coffee buddies.

But there, sitting close to a cheap-paneling wall, with odds and ends of decoration all over it, was my know-it-all sister, acting in her normally ungraceful way. She asked Jerome, "What makes you think that the Bible the mortician gave you was my brother's?"

Jerome didn't say a word; he just opened the front cover for my kid sister to see. Inside the cover, she saw a date—July 10, 1968—and it read: "On this day that I prayed that my sister would live [my sister had to recognize the day. It was when she had broken her neck when that young black gelding threw her], I accept the One I prayed to as my own Lord and Savior."

Then my signature was there as I had always signed when I was a child, bold and smooth, as I was taught to write cursive in grade school, and with my middle name.

2

'50 Buick Radio

I want some red roses for a blue lady,
Send them to the fairest gal in town ...[1]

The lyrics soothed five head of milk cows standing patiently in stanchions. The stanchions restrained the cows' heads from moving side to side, while still able to lower or raise their heads. Maybe they were able to twist their necks to see the other milk cows eating their portion of grain, which was a mixture of wheat and milo or corn, but the cows ate contentedly and were not really interested in what their fellow cows were doing. The cows stood still, knowing, due to their experience, that this milking was just for a moment. Other than the occasional stomping of the hooves and swishing of their tails at either biting or imaginary flies, they stood still while we drained their bags of milk.

The song was sung by a man with a smooth country voice; he was without a physical image and was accompanied by a single accordion pulsating from an old 1950 Buick radio. It was automotive-equipment black, a color that was used to give metal protection from rust, and larger than any modern radio, especially with the introduction of so many personal electronic devices that many homes no longer have a

---

[1] Adapted lyrics from "Red Roses for a Blue Lady" were written by Sid Tepper and Roy Brodsky.

radio in view. It stood nearly the size of an antique tabletop radio, from the beginning of the radio technology, yet without the pointed cathedral shape and ornamentation of wood scrolls with which the younger generation have no connection. This gigantic music maker had a rather large speaker built in it, making its one-piece design ideal for use out of the car.

During the early sixties, the old Buick was no longer in use and sat with weeds growing up around it. The radio was salvaged by our farm family's two eldest boys after a discussion with our father about the fact that it still worked and the battery in the car was not very old. Once the radio was free from the confines of the unused car, a scrap piece of a two-by-six board was nailed between two studs of the milk barn's supporting wall. The radio was then centered on the wood plank and gave the sound machine a performing platform. The Buick's antenna cable and antenna was then stretched up into the overhead of the barn and laid alongside a rafter where one could see the cedar shingles from below stretching from wood slat board to wood slat board. The antenna was held in place by a pair of rusty fencing staples, dug out of an old tin coffee can that held odds and ends. Everything in the tin can was used, and the rusty staples had to be straightened out, since they had been pulled out of a pasture's wood fence post. Another crude two-by-six was positioned below the radio to hold the reclaimed eight-volt car battery. The battery that had powered an entire car now became the power for the old radio. This was suitable and economical for calming our dairy cattle. The milk cows were much easier to milk if they were calm, rather than stomping around nervously.

On our Midwestern farm, milking cows was a family affair, with father, mother, brothers, and sisters steadily stripping warm milk into tin pails. Sometimes, the chore seemed to be a burden, but then sometimes, it was simply good to be all together, talking and laughing at whatever, as we shared the toil. Whatever the case, the '50 Buick radio stilled the sometimes nervous milk cows. Or, its music filled the emptiness of the air and provided a backdrop for all the happenings in the milk barn.

***

9

Decades later, a man reached up to remove the long-unused '50 Buick radio from its dusty shelf. He dusted it off with his bare hands and smiled. He then climbed up on a barely trustworthy wooden ladder that he had found discarded off to the side; he remembered using it when he was younger and lighter as the ladder rungs sponged under his weight. He pried the staples out of the rafter with an old screwdriver that had been left on a decaying table, and the antenna came loose from the rafters. The antenna was still shiny, being made from true stainless steel rather than the alloy that is now passed off as stainless steel, which will rust in time. He looked at the battery, but it didn't look good. He pried off the caps where distilled water was supposed to cover the electro-plates that stored the electricity. He saw a lot of corrosion on the dry plates and decided that the battery was not worth taking. The radio, however, looked okay and was working when the barn was last used; he thought it might still work.

This balding man had been the eldest of those farm kids and one of the two boys moving the radio years earlier from the car to the milk barn. He thought about the days when he was part of the milking family, working to the beat of the old-style country music. The steady beat of milk squirting in the bottom of the empty buckets gave an amplified growl that dulled as the fluid level rose, changing it into a rhythmic beat. The rhythm of the family work was a generous accompaniment to the Buick's donated tunes. The middle-aged man fondly remembered how the real music was made by family toil and activities, and how the AM radio, for thirty years, provided background music without a channel change.

During the week, it was the same man singing and telling jokes between the news, weather, and farm reports. On Sunday mornings, there were the gospel greats. And we all knew these songs and could sing them from memory. We had sung all these songs many times in our little church, which sat on the side of a country sand road, just a little ways away up and over the hills.

The evenings were the recorded music from the music artists of that day—the one he remembered as being his favorite was Sonny James. "Young Love" streamed through his head for just a moment, and then he placed his treasure in the backseat of his four-door truck. He chuckled at the memory of how much smaller the 1949 Chevy truck had been that he'd driven around this farm.

It grieved him to see the farm in a state of disrepair and the buildings unused. This was the yard where, as a lanky boy, he had learned a good work ethic and how to build hot rods. It was where he brought his shy life's love to meet his parents, and he remembered how their secure love was once a young love. Yet those days lived in his mind and heart and not in the abandoned farmyard. The radio was just one piece of the past, reminding him of his youthful memories.

At his home, he cleaned the old AM radio, gently blew dust out of it with dried and regulated air, and reworked the piece, stimulating his memory. He replaced the speaker, as the original speaker's diaphragm was rotten from age. His face was a mixture of hope and worry when he hooked up the extending wires to a battery using vise-grip pliers to secure the stripped wires to the round battery post of a battery. He was taking a chance, not knowing if the radio would work, when he purchased the eight-volt battery at a tractor-part supply store. The Buick had been an eight-volt system and nothing but an older, small tractor used an eight-volt battery in this day and age.

The hot wire was connected first, as always, and then the ground wire was clamped on second. His heart danced and was joyously amazed when a crackle spurted out of the speaker, and then music streamed, once it was dialed in to one of the few remaining AM radio stations in the area. Fittingly, the AM radio station he found was a farm radio station. Soon, in his excitement, he was nailing up an old two-by-six between two studs of the wall of his workshop to mount the radio. His face beamed, and his deep-set eyes shone with sparkles under his bushy eyebrows as the task reached completion, with the radio, battery, and antenna all in place, just as they had existed on the farm.

On the wall of his plumbing workshop stood a connection—the radio was a connection to family and childhood. Life had come full circle. Maybe no one else was able to understand his fascination and delight in such an obsolete radio, as most of the world now listened to iPods and FM or XM radios, but then, the world didn't need to understand, because it was something felt and not intellectually comprehended. The thoughts and memories were his alone, and he knew that if he tried to explain what the radio meant to him, he would end up saying, "I guess you had to be there." Therefore, he was silent about the radio. He had a good vibration in his chest, a flutter in his heart, and a spiritual comfort, something unspoken, experienced, and personal.

***

Several decades later, a man reached up to remove the long unused 1950 Buick AM radio from its dusty shelf in his father's workshop. The man never understood his father's interest in such a bulky old radio, yet he fondly remembered working in the workshop with his father to its crackling. Songs poured out to fill gaps in conversation, accompanied rhythms of ratchets and banging wenches or hammers, while he and his father gathered materials and tools to do a job together, build a hot rod, or repair a family vehicle. Those were good times. He pondered as he held it in his hands. "I wonder if this old radio still works. I could use a radio in my garage."

3

A Gift

This morning God offered me a gift:
Robins were feeding in my yard,
Small blackbirds cooperatively built their nest,
Crows swooped by,
Sparrows flitted through the air,
Huge hawks rested on the breeze,
My heart beat within my chest,
God has shown me His presence.

4

A True Gift

My arms grew heavy, my aching legs tingled, and exhaustion pushed me down as I sorted meat scraps, the good from the bad. The meat came down the conveyor belt it great heaps. I shoved the stacks of meat out, level within the sides of the conveyor belt and looked for the scraps that were mostly meat. I worked with other women who either spoke an Asian language or Spanish, and after all these years, I could only pick out a word once in a while. They talked among themselves. Once in a while, they would try to tell me something, and I would smile at them in my ignorance of their language.

The belt ran on forever without ending. The beef-packing plant ran 480 head through every hour, I have been told, when the managers in their pride boasted at those meeting that I had to suffer. The cattle came in bawling at one end and were loaded onto waiting semi-trucks on the other end of the plant, frozen and neatly packed in cardboard boxes. The cattle were helpless in the lanes and chutes as they headed for slaughter, which I saw every morning and evening on my way in and out of this plant. I looked down the racing conveyor and wondered at the heaps I saw coming at me. It seemed that all my joints ached when my shift finally ended.

I was glad my time on the belt was finished but dreaded the long walk down the corridor, across the concrete lot with semi-trucks and forklifts roaring by, to the guard shack and then out to the middle of the parking lot, built to park five hundred cars, so it seemed. The walk was long and miserable, but thanks to the good Lord, there was a break room located off the hallway on the way out of the building, so I could rest for a few moments before I went on.

The young folks who worked with me at the plant had so much energy; they swished by while they talked and joked without acknowledging my presence. Seems hardly anyone ever made eye contact or spoke to me. I tried to make friends among them and to get to know them, but it was rare that one of them took the time to do more than answer my comments or question, if they acknowledged me at all. I guess I did look funny in my thrift-shop clothes. The double-knit that was available at the local thrift shops was always the cheapest and most convenient way to clothe myself—I can't be finicky in my income bracket and with my bills. I was always able to find double-knit slacks that I could enlarge by ripping out the outer seam and sewing material from other double-knit slacks in the sides. I was thankful for clothing, and a person in my situation couldn't be particular about how the colors looked together. Maybe my slacks had some kind of floral design—or something close to that—with a solid color up the side, or vice versa. Sometimes they were both of patterns, but not the same kind.

Well, anyway I had clothes, and I was thankful for that. God has always made sure that I had clothes, meals, and home. I thought about my times as a child, living on the Arkansas River, when Mom washed my clothes while I bathed because there was nothing else for me to wear. I wrapped in a blanket until my clothes were dry from the summer breeze or from the heat off the woodstove. In remembering those times, I prayed, "I thank you, Jesus, for my clothing and home." Christmas wasn't much back then, yet we didn't know that some folks had more, because all the folks that we knew didn't have any more than we did. Fruit and candies were a special treat when Santa came. But that was a time when, out of necessity, we grew almost all our food or caught it in the river.

These days, I was thankful for enough clothes that my laundry could always be put off a week before I ran out of anything to wear. Well, if I had the money to buy my clothes at the so-called discount stores, they wouldn't have anything in my size anyway.

I saw the youngsters around me exchanging gifts in the hallway. They called out to each other, "Merry Christmas," and "See you at the dance on New Year's Eve," and the like. I understood how they liked having the time off from work for good moments with their families, but I wished I could work straight through the holidays and forget about Christmas, New Year's Eve, and the whole shebang. It would be better for me if I could earn more money to pay the bills, rather than take time off.

At home, I had my youngest children and all my grandchildren living with me. My son had lost his legs in an accident at the same beef-packing house where I worked. It had happened in the middle of the night; about twenty feet from where I sorted meat scraps, and horrifying thoughts ran through my mind often, as I pushed myself to focus on the task at hand. He had been inside a huge meat auger with a high-pressure hot-water hose, washing the fat that clung to everything like Play-Doh. My meat scraps traveled down conveyor belts then into this meat auger which fed the hopers of the hamburger machines. A maintenance man turned on the meat auger to check his repairs on its gearbox, not realizing that anyone was inside of it. When the auger came on my son's legs became meat—the machine didn't know or feel a thing. The maintenance man turned off the auger as quickly as he was able when he heard my son's screams. I could tell when he later apologized to me that he was horrified when he looked in the auger, but by that time, my son had no legs. I supposed we should be glad for his life, and I am. I am his mother, yet my insides go numb when I think about it.

He did receive some money after the lawyers got what they called their share, but soon the money ran out, and when the money was gone, so was my daughter-in-law. He had nothing at that point, and it wouldn't have been right to have my son and grandkids in a homeless shelter after they were evicted from their apartment; I brought them home to live with me. At that point, my son didn't seem to want to do anything. He said he couldn't work without legs, and so he didn't try. Some people called it depression, but what did I know? Seemed to me the solution was to do something—anything—yet it was hard for me to say anything when I looked at him in his wheelchair. When I did try to talk to him, it went nowhere, and he didn't make a lot of sense in what he had to say.

Therefore, I did what I knew how to do and went to work as much as possible.

With all my family in my home, my paycheck didn't always cover all the bills and expenses. The children's schools would twenty-dollars a person to death, with this or that activity or function. I had heard that God said a person who didn't take care of his family was worse than an infidel. Well, even if He didn't say it, I would have taken care of my kids and grandkids anyway.

I thought on those things as I stepped down the hallway, reconfirming my resolve to keep walking every time the soles of my feet tingled and to keep working to see us all through these times. I found the door to the break room and sat in the nearest booth. My heart hung heavy inside my chest, like it would fall out if there was a slit for it to tumble out. I thought about my family and the little hard-earned money that we had. I couldn't rest long, but a few minutes wouldn't hurt … I guessed.

A young couple came by, and I wished them a merry Christmas. They smiled and returned the greeting as they rushed by. They were so young and never seemed to get along, which, to me, was crazy. I thought that anything could be worked out if people really wanted to work it out. They were both nice, but he was the one who would occasionally take time to chat with me. The few sentences of polite conversation would help me to relax and rest for a moment and forget my troubles.

After I relaxed a little, I steadied myself and then moved to the door and down the corridor. I didn't move as fast as those around me, but I only stopped once, and that was to tighten my scarf over my head before I stepped out into the cold. I didn't need to get sick with a cold or anything else.

Pam, the lead man—well, lead lady in this case—on my crew nearly bumped into me as she hurried past me. She kept her focus on the girls she was chatting with, who giggled and trotted on past me. I always thought it odd how people would listen to a pretty young lady with no experience as though she was Plato or a Fortune 500 CEO, but they would not pay any attention to a person with experience. I observed them as they let the door slam shut behind them—it almost slammed in my face, without the young ladies noticing that I was there. When someone doesn't want to be your friend, that is okay and understandable, but rudeness is something else.

With one hand on the handrail and the other on the door handle, I pushed the door open, and the cold air crystallized my face. The steps I needed to descend had spots of ice, even though they had been scooped clear of the snow, and my careful steps threw sharp pains into my hips and knees. The walk to my car also was slick from snow melting and then refreezing. This late in the afternoon, the temperature had dropped, and the melted snow was already forming into ice. I walked slowly—at least I must have been slow, judging by the speed that everyone else was speeding by me. The still-frigid air was stinging cold. The door of my battered Dodge Valiant (not looking very valiant) groaned when I pulled it open. I thought, *I must oil those hinges one of these days.* My husband used to take care of these things. Missing him was an understatement. I tossed my handbag across the ripped vinyl seat. I dreaded putting out the effort required to squeeze under the steering wheel.

The engine turned over frightfully slow but then grunted to life. I drove home, with bill collectors on my mind, knowing there wasn't much tread on my tires. I would never cheat anyone and certainly wanted to pay my bills, yet the people collecting didn't care about my income and outgo. Some of the creditors had been knocking on my door, asking for money, and it was money I didn't have. These were not debts for frivolous things but for keeping hot running water in my house and for children's doctor visits and such. I don't remember what all the expenses were, but they were all to keep a reasonable house. If a person didn't keep all the utilities functioning and the house in good repair, then there were some folks who could really cause trouble when there were kids in the house.

I hadn't had enough money to pay all my bills for months. It had been hard enough to feed everyone in my house and, darn it, today was Christmas Eve. The decorations that I drove past every day, and the Christmas carols I heard over various speakers seemed thin, hollow, and out of place—they seemed unreal. I just kept thinking how the little ones were expecting gifts from Santa. It was all I could do to provide one basic meal on Christmas Day—our meal would be simple, but we would eat.

My tires spun on the hard-packed snow as I drove into my driveway—new tires would be nice. One of the children must have shoveled a narrow walkway from the driveway to the front door, and for that I was thankful. My two-story house seemed too small as I walked up to it. It had once been a beautiful home. When my husband was alive, he had earned a nice living and kept everything in good repair, and I'd had time to plant flowers. At this point, my house needed a coat of paint and tender loving care. Now, even the taxes were a heavy burden. American ownership didn't seem like much when the same government could take someone's only home because taxes were due.

Carefully, I stepped up the steps that I no longer trusted, and grasped the handrail that needed a couple of more screws added to it. The lid of the mailbox squawked out its need for replacement or oil on its hinge. I hoped that there weren't any bills in it, but there were. A Christmas card would have been nice, but even Job's friends left him when times got hard, according to the Book.

The front room was a wreck when I stepped into it. Charlie, my three-year-old granddaughter, sat cross-legged on the floor and too close to the TV. Innocently, she gave me a beautiful smile and a "Hi, Nana." My teenage daughter was absorbed in a magazine and lounged among a mess of assorted teen magazines on the sofa—a piece of furniture that I would have liked to have replaced long ago. I patted her head on the way by because she wouldn't have heard me speak over her headphones. The others were scattered throughout the house. The kind of music that kids listen to these days was blasting down from the upstairs. *Too loud*, I thought, but I was too tired to say so. I moved to the kitchen and sat down at the table to relax for a moment. I sat numb, and the stress of the workday clung to the back of my neck and shoulders the way a raccoon holds onto a tree branch when hunting dogs are below, clawing and howling at him. I needed the stress to leave; darn the dogs.

I had told the children that there might not be much of a Christmas this year, yet the little ones were excited about Santa's coming during the night. They didn't realize that the generosity of Santa was tied directly to the financial situation of the head of the household. I had hoped that something would happen and even said a prayer about it. I wanted to buy the little ones each a little gift, but even the dollar store's toys were unobtainable. The weight settled on me as I remembered the times as a child when I wanted more, but not much was there. Yet I never had a time like this before—not in childhood or adulthood. There had always been something for everyone at Christmas.

I had been sitting for what seemed like only a moment, wishing for more energy, when an explosion of knocking came on the front door, startling me from my heavy thoughts. *Those darn bill collectors have a lot nerve to harass me on Christmas Eve*, I thought as my hidden frustration swelled. I pushed myself up, and sharp pains shot through my feet. Failure hung all over me, thick and heavy, as I moved to the door. I would tell this one a thing or two, I decided, because what kind of a person would ask for money on Christmas Eve?

I pulled back the curtain on the window in the door, but I couldn't see anyone outside. *He's probably standing off to the side*, I thought, *as sneaky people sometimes do.* I tugged the inside door open but still saw no one. I pushed on the storm door, but it moved only a little before it warped out slightly—the bottom of it was restricted. I pushed my face up against the glass in the storm door and saw that a large cardboard box was against the door. I tried to shove against it, but the box wouldn't move. My daughter lifted her eyes from what she was reading, pushed her headphones off, and watched me. I asked her to go around through the back door and move the box that prevented me from opening the door.

As teenagers do, she sprinted out the back door and around the house, without even bothering to put on a jacket, much to my displeasure. "I don't need another doctor bill when she gets sick," I grumbled to myself. When she reached the box and lifted its flaps to look inside, she squealed something I couldn't understand. Impatiently, I said, "Move the box, child!" She pushed the box over with both hands on it, as if she was pushing a car out of a snowbank, and I stepped outside to see what she was squealing and chattering about.

It was unbelievable, but just like the unreal Christmas decorations that were really there, so were there unbelievable items really in the box.

The box was stuffed, full to the brim. Wonderfully full of food and carefully wrapped gifts, each gift was tagged with a name of each child in the house. Santa (or someone) had come. There was a large turkey, a ham, some canned goods, a sack of sweet potatoes—more than was needed for a family Christmas dinner. Pushing and pulling, we relocated the bounty inside our now wonderful home. My kids were really helpful in sorting through the blessings, and warmness engulfed me—the way you feel when someone gives you a much-needed hug, the kind of hug that lets the stress drop away and leaves a smile within that can be felt all though your being. My son had wheeled over to join us, and his face looked younger.

The message of being loved was the most prized gift in the box. In those few moments of time, our world was transformed. There was no lack. My body felt lively.

This box held more than toys for children and food for a family. It held the true gift: a generous measure of hope.

5

Badger

On a short pew sat three young boys in a small country church. These boys were brothers in every way. They fought each other over the smallest things, shared with each other, and defended each other. Together, they could dream up the darnedest things; what one didn't think of, the other did. Their being "active" would have been an understatement. Ever since the boys were able to walk, they found ways to frustrate their mother with their things-to-do list.

On this pew they were dreaming up things to do in the hills of their father's farm. This farm was just the place for boys to live and play. Why, there were imaginary black bears, grizzly bears, giraffes, and cougars, not to mention the lost tribe of Indians who camped up the draw in the trees or the stray Nazi soldiers that somehow found their way to the private hills. The boys had to deal with hazards, but they were happy to do it.

They sat with the rest of their family on this hardwood pew; mother and father sat in the middle, watching intently so no one dared to misbehave. Sitting was a very difficult job for these youngsters; especially on this bright summer morning, with excited thoughts spinning through their minds. Because within the largest playground those three young boys could ever have, they were sure that they could trap one of the wild animals living in trees, bushes, and holes—for real this time. Their youthful imaginations were fed by the monthly arrival of *Boys' Life* magazine, which encouraged the boys to hunt, fish, and trap wild animals.

Often, the boys had wondered at the steel-spring traps hanging in their father's workshop. The traps were a mechanical marvel, the power of which was demonstrated to them by a wiser older brother, who warned them that they could lose a finger in the trap, and it would be cut off forever if they ever dared to touch it. Big brother even demonstrated its strange power by setting the trap and snapping a stick in it. But that didn't deter the boys and then, nudged by the promise of wonderful furs, they thought about it and talked about the danger of the traps.

"Remember how he put his foot on the jaws of the trap once it was open to hold it?"

"Yeah, and there are two of us to hold the trap while the other sets the tab."

With that, it was decided that the boys were able to handle the traps, and soon they told their dreams to their father. His dark brown eyes shone with sparkles of humor while the boys stated their request to be trappers, and he chuckled with remembrances of his own childhood adventures. The threesome had heard stories of their father's trapping episodes, his being different because times were harder when he was a boy. He and his family had survived the "Dirty Thirties," and the furs helped to put food on the table for his family during the hard times. The boys' father was the oldest son in his family, though he had an older sister, and he did everything he could to make life easier for his mother and siblings. In comparison, these boys' biggest problem was trying to ignore the Beatles and Elvis that their older brothers and sister kept talking about.

The boys explained to their father that they had found the best hole in a bank of, where a critter good for trapping surely lived ("Rabbit," six-year-old youngest brother insisted). The breed of the animal was not as important to his two brothers, who were just a few years older. They wished for beaver pelts, but since there were no beaver dams or continually flowing creeks in the vicinity, beaver pelts seemed unlikely. Many articles in *Boys' Life* magazine had educated the youngsters about beaver dams, the streams where beaver lived, and how to trap them. Yet after some serious discussion between the boys, who stood in an erect line, and their father, who sat at the head of the dining table drinking a mid-morning cup of coffee, permission was humorously given to use one of his steel traps. "Can you get it down?" Father asked.

"Yup!" was their battle cry in unison.

Now, with boyish determination, the break of day found them skirting around a pond filled with bullhead fish and hiking up a tree-lined draw to the predetermined land of promise—to the rabbit hole that was in a dirt bank up a narrow ravine, a ways above the pond. It was no wonder that the boys found this hole, as it was in route to a junk pile where lots of treasure was found, such as old bottles and rusty horseshoes. And this was where the young trappers thought there just had to be a critter sleeping the day away, while waiting for the night to bring his world into action.

They knew from school lessons that many animals slept during the day and roamed at night, and then there was *The Bugs Bunny Show* that they saw every Saturday morning, which taught the fallacy that rabbits lived in holes in the ground. Therefore, this was the place to begin, even though there was no sign outside the hole, declaring it to be a rabbit residence.

The plan was to place the trap in the entrance of the hole that was tunneled horizontally back into the bank, leaving no way for the rabbit to pass without getting a furry foot caught in its steel jaws. It was like stacking a deck of poker cards, making the win certain. The worry was, after their older brother's stick demonstration, that the rabbit's foot would be cut off and the intended prey would hop off with one foot left behind, like lizards leave their wiggling tails behind—as when the boys tried to grab them. But big brother came to the rescue again when questioned. "Oh, don't worry! The trap is made to catch animals and hold them without cutting the foot off," explained their lofty sibling.

When they had finished securely driving a steel stake into the ground through the ring at the end of the chain, which was attached to the trap, they knew their plan was flawless—no way could they fail at catching this coveted rabbit.

All through supper and that evening, the assured reward to come fully occupied the boys' minds, as well as what they would do with their fine fur. They weren't sure how to skin a rabbit, but it hadn't been that long ago that they had walked up to the mile road west of the farmhouse to skin off a pair of coyote ears, along with the strip of hide between the ears, for the bounty placed on the coyotes. Coyotes overpopulated the area in those days and were thought to be a menace to the domestic livestock. Their dad had told them where the fallen coyote lay and that they needed the ears with the piece of hide between them to keep the ears together. It wasn't that long of a walk for these adventurers, who were always on their feet to some undertaking or another. The mile road was three-quarters of a mile away from the barnyard, which wasn't far—except when a person considered all the crevices in the hills to be explored and imaginary challenges that had to be dealt with along the way. Those things made it a much longer trip, but in the end, they got the bounty money.

Time always seems to move slowly for the young and it did especially for these three. They woke often to look at the window to see if they could see the early morning glow. Yet no matter how long the hours until dawn, the sun did finally rise the next morning on schedule, casting a new light on the only hills the boys had ever known. The chores were done with speed such as no one had ever seen on this farm, freeing up the young trappers to run their one trap. Their dad smiled a knowing smile, without saying a word, and he chuckled within his spirit.

Upon arrival at the rabbit hole, the threesome was pleased to see that the trap was out of sight and farther in the hole. Also, the chain was tight, which also promised wild game, but the boys were perplexed when the oldest brother, who was strong because he was nine years old, couldn't pull the trap out of the hole. They knew that a rabbit should have been easy to pull out into the open because they did have tame rabbits that they cared for in cages and the tame rabbits they could easily pull out of their cages. But the strongest of the trio couldn't make the chain come out of the hole; so the boy who was in the middle in age lent a hand, grabbing hold of the chain and then cooperatively pulling in sync with his older brother. This caused them to gain a little more slack in the chain but not bring out the rabbit; and when they let go, it jerked back into the hole as if a huge rubber band was attached to the other end.

The answer was obvious: the youngest brother also needed to put his strength to the chain. They were pleased to see that their combined efforts caused the chain to start coming out of the little cave, but they were shocked upon finding themselves high on the opposite bank, looking down at a snarling gray animal, with lots of sharp teeth generously displayed as a warning for the boys to stay back. It wasn't that clear to the boys how they went from pulling on the chain to standing high up out of reach, but that wasn't really important at this point.

"What's that?" screamed the littlest one with a small index finger aimed and trembling. There came a quick answer from both of his brothers: "A *badger!*"

What to do now dominated the trio's minds. That critter would really hurt them if they tried to get hold on him. This was not a rabbit with a little strength but an animal able to defend itself and to take down other animals. Therefore, in only a few seconds their effective imaginations canceled the idea of grabbing him. Besides, it didn't take much imagination to understand the damage that the badger could do to their bodies when watching the critter tear up the dirt and display long claws and teeth that seemed to be extremely sharp. All they had to do was remember how the friendly barn cats' claws felt when they decided to sink their claws in the flesh of an arm or hand.

After a few minutes of discussion, the answer was obvious: "We need the rifle." Then, as fast as they could go, they headed for the house. They never made better time than they did that day—no distractions as they ran down the draw, around the pond (not even slowing to skip a rock), over the hill, and under the barbed-wire cattle gate. Then, just as they came around the huge mulberry tree in front of the farmhouse, their dad poked his head out of the workshop. Their excited chatter and racing feet had alerted their father that something was up, and he asked, "You boys catch something?"

"Sure did," responded the eldest, "and we need the rifle because we caught us a mean old badger."

I imagine it didn't seem safe to send three excited boys off together with one rifle, so Dad had to have been laughing on the inside when, with a straight face, he told the three boys, "I always hit what I caught in the head with a hammer. Rifle shells cost too much."

The young kids, not understanding that a heavy hammer was required to put a dent in the skull of a snarling badger, were back on their tough mission, with a light nail hammer in hand. They took turns carrying the hammer, like relay runners, though the hammer was only heavy enough to really upset a trapped badger. They didn't know what a badger skin was worth, but that could be found out later.

The hammer plan had one other flaw—a person had to get awful close to that mean, snarling badger to hit him in the head. All of the sudden the hammer's handle seemed to be the short straw.

The oldest of the three boys and the most courageous was the first to plunk the wary critter smack on the top of the head. The snarling badger threw dirt with his four claws and jumped all over at the end of the weak-looking chain. At this point, the boys were reminded of the Tasmanian Devil (one of Bugs Bunny's friends). The boys didn't have to worry about the animal darting out at them when one of them approached him, with the hammer extended as far as possible in order to put the badger out. This was because at the very sight of the boys, the whirlwind of meanness was at the end of the chain, displaying a many-toothed threat. The badger was always far out toward the obvious threat to him, which was the boys. And the badger displayed as much of a threat as he was able to show in self-preservation. Slowly, the eldest would sneak up on him, if one could sneak up on such an angry critter, and then smack him as close to square on the head as a scared pair of young hands on a light hammer could. Then he'd run back onto the waiting security of the opposite dirt bank. There seemed to be safety in the numbers of his brothers. Imagine their disappointment when the badger was still very much awake after being smacked with the heaviest blow the toughest brother could come up with.

What would anyone do who was getting pinged on the head with a hammer, let alone a badger who didn't like humans in the first place? He'd do his best to hurt someone. Isn't that reasonable? The boys thought that was just what the badger was thinking; because this badger seemed to know that it was just a matter of tugging the stake loose from the dirt at the end of the chain and then chewing on some boy's legs. He jerked, pulled, and shook around, doing his best to pull out the restricting stake, while the boys sat watching and pulling their knees close to their chests.

The boys, not being born yesterday, had noticed that the critter was close to pulling the stake out of the ground and thus getting loose so he could chew their legs into stumps. They didn't realize that the animal just wanted to get away from them and wasn't interested in much else. With their limited knowledge, they decided that it was time to resubmit their request for a firearm. They really didn't know what else to do, as the situation looked very dire. If they were not able to take this badger, then they would be failures on their first trapping venture, and that just wouldn't due.

Again, the boys stood up straight in front of their dad. They were as serious as any set of kids could be, with wide-open eyes and flushed cheeks, submitting their desire to be allowed to shoot the mean old thing with the rifle. The rifle was an old bolt-action single-shot with a long barrel; it was the only gun their father would let them shoot. Even though it had a long barrel, it was fairly light, with its lack of mechanisms.

"Who's going to do the shootin'?" their father asked as he turned a wrench on a bolt of the sickle-bar hay mower. Then, finally, after a lot of instruction about where the barrel would be pointed as they walked and questions about who was going to carry and use the rifle, there came the instructions. The oldest and most experienced of the boys was the obvious choice for handling the gun; after all, he was nine years old, and while his brothers argued that each boy was just as able as the other, they agreed, and permission to take the rifle and end this little war was given.

Then the boys ran hard, with their chests out and pumping arms—that is, all except the eldest, who held the rifle up in front and trotted as if he were an army soldier, running across a war-torn battlefield—indeed, in his mind and heart, that is where he ran and existed. They skirted the hill toward the bullhead-infested pond, and if they would have had eyes in the backs of their heads, they would have seen their father watching them run as he sat on the mower and laughed. What he was laughing about, one couldn't be sure, because he never said. Was it the excitement of his boys? Was it the thought of their brand new adventure? Or was it his boyhood memories—memories like we all hold back from telling because we all think that someone had to "be there" to appreciate them? These things are what make a person chuckle from deep within himself when his own children's behaviors bring to the surface his own childhood memories.

The boys didn't even look sideways at the pond as they ran past it and on up the draw, toward the little ravine that was at the trail's end. They noticed every detail as they ran, but they didn't take their eyes or focus off the mission, and everything began to slow. It was as if the sun had stopped moving as they approached the rabbit hole that had turned into a monster hole. Then, the now-armed and much braver three stood in a semi-shock state and looked. They had been ready for battle ... but there was no war. There was the hole—a hole where the stake had been driven—and claw marks all over the ground. They weren't dreaming that the badger had been there. Yet it was now just a hole, for there was no badger or trap. The chain and stake were gone too—everything. They looked up and down the little draw—nothing.

Then the boys decided that the badger must have gone deep into the hole, hiding the chain within the depths of its caverns. Just to make sure, though, they found a long stick and jammed it as far as they could into the hole. They then realized that it wasn't that deep because they could hit the back of the little cave. Now this was a dilemma.

"Where is he?" the youngest of the three almost screamed. They were all thinking the same thing: "Where is he hiding and ready to bite us?" Well, nothing happened, and all was quiet as they whirled around, looking for their attacker.

Looking up and down the ravine, they decided that if there had been a place for the badger to hide in the lower part of the ravine, they would have seen it on their way up. That left the boys to go up higher to look for another hole in the draw. They hadn't gone far when they saw movement under some tree roots that had grown across the ravine, holding back a bank of dirt and giving any animal that was daring a shelter of sorts. Again, they were extremely alert, holding the rifle out in front, remembering the threat that the badger had held against them with his teeth.

The chain was dangling out in the open again, giving the youngsters an opportunity to try to tug him out from under the tree roots so they could put an end to this strange situation. The badger was trying to distance himself from the pestering humans, who were determined to make his life miserable, if not short. Consequently, he had wrapped the chain in a maze around the roots making it impossible for the three, even in a joint effort, to pull him out into the sunlight.

This project became tiring really fast, so then they had to put their heads together for a new plan. It didn't take long for them to decide to shoot him where he was. This brought about a real show, had someone been there to watch the three prepare to execute the innocent, accused animal, while within his cell of root bars.

The eldest boy gave orders for everyone to stand back, and the two younger brothers stepped one step back, forming a short line of attention. The show began. The eldest boy raised the single-shot bolt-action rifle, with his chest out, and his back straight, and the firing squad prepared. With a drum-roll beat within the boys' heads (or was it the rapid beating of their hearts?), with one shot, he killed a root.

This was disappointing, but the execution wasn't over. It was time to take some sort of action because the badger, not liking the sunlight, was doing his best to stay in the shadows and alive. By this time, the sun was coming up high, and the day was bright. The boys, with their squinted eyes, peered under the dirt-and-grass roof that covered the root system and saw red eyes staring back at them from behind some crooked roots. Here was the answer; all they had to do was aim at the red eyes, and the varmint was done for.

Mark was glad that he had grabbed a couple of extra bullets (against his father's instruction to take only one). "Because if a man can shoot, one bullet is all he really needs"—this was their father's instruction, something he had said many times. But in Mark's inexperience, the two extra shells were a blessing, because now, another one was needed to finish the job.

He was careful this time because he already would have to explain why he had to shoot twice, knowing that his dad would be listening from over the hill in the farmyard. There were no loud noises in the rolling hills, so their father would hear any extra or unusual noise, without his even focusing on it. Yes, after close inspection the second shot did the job ... of killing another root. The badger was canny and had crawled behind a larger root, as if he knew what was about to happen. But luckily (or by wisdom), they still had one more bullet—that was sure to do the job.

To see the badger's eyes, the young man had to get closer in toward the bank of dirt-covered tree roots, which really made him uncomfortable, as he remembered the critter's ferociousness. His brothers stood, not so much at attention but bent over with some doubt this time. The rifle barrel waved and bobbed more this time, but determination dwelt in the furrows of the rifleman's forehead. The rifle cracked, but the boys didn't see any splinters fly off the roots.

Excitement burst out of the boys, but as they looked, they couldn't see a badger; the kill couldn't be confirmed. Retrieving the badger and trap was still a problem. The chain came out where they could get a hold on it and tug, but nothing budged. The chain was wrapped around the tree roots, and the brave three weren't daring enough to reach into the dark of the root shelter and unwrap it. They knew the badger was still there because the chain was there, as was the trap with the animal at the end of it.

The boys hurried home, not so fast this time. They also had another problem; it was time to return to the barnyard without the badger or trap and with three empty shell casings, which they dutifully had picked up. They knew they wouldn't have to tell their father how many times they had shot the rifle—he already knew—but the lacking trap and badger was a terrible problem. They didn't look so proud when they stood in line in front of their father this time, as they explained their adventure.

"I've had that trap for longer than the three of you boys have lived altogether," their father reprimanded. The boys shifted and pushed their hands to the bottom of their pants pockets, and their chins were against their chests. "Give me the rifle," he said, and Mark handed it out. Their father walked into the house, and the boys looked at each other.

The boy's failure was too much to bear. Their father was disappointed in them, and they had failed. They wandered around the farm over the next couple of days, avoiding the ravine of failure. They worked on their coaster, which they rode down the hill next to the farmhouse, as it was a good distraction, and when they needed a hammer, the middle son went into the workshop to retrieve one of their father's.

As the boy grabbed the hammer off the workbench, something else almost fell off, and he grabbed it quickly. His eyes opened wide and sparkled. He ran to his brothers with both hands full, crying, "Let's cut him out!"

"What?"

The boy held up a small tree-branch saw, and the coaster was soon forgotten. The boys were on their feet and skirting the hill next to the house, in a big hurry.

Nothing stirred within the roots, but the chain was still there. They cut loose this root and that root, sawing until they thought their skinny arms would fall off from fatigue. The sun was approaching the line of hilltops in the west when they finally had cut enough roots to reach the trap. Yes, the trap, yet there was no badger. The badger was as canny as he was fierce and had somehow freed himself from the steel trap, which had a thick root wedged in it, holding it open. The boys looked everywhere up into the roots, but there was no animal of any kind—and they could see all the way back to the dirt bank, once they cut back the root system. There was no badger. But they had the trap, and the boys remembered that their father hadn't said anything about the nonexistent badger but only about his lost steel trap.

Their father sat at the kitchen table in his bib overalls, his cap sitting next to his cup of coffee. His dark hair was full and combed back, and he watched with steady dark eyes as the boys let the wood-framed screen door slam behind them. The middle boy held the trap up high. His two comrades were on either side of him, and it was hard to say who was first to tell their father they had retrieved the trap. There wasn't any mention of where they would trap next. Their father's eyes twinkled as he said, "I supposed you can reach the nail where it hangs as easily as you did to get it down."

And that is how we three successful boys became unsuccessful trappers.

6

Don't Mess with Success

"Let's go to Mexico." Jose was insistent about my going with him. He continued as I hesitated, while I looked out into nothing. "I know you have vacation time coming. You never take time off from work and it's about time you did." I gazed out across the beef-packing plant parking lot, thinking that I had never been to Mexico or many other places, other than the eastern slope of the Rocky Mountains. Life had taken unexpected, bad turns for me recently, and I was feeling overwhelmed.

Jose continued, "We will go to my parents' house. There are no motels or any other places to stay in my hometown. It is just different where we are going. We can take turns driving on the way—it is a little over twenty-six hours to my hometown from here and my wife doesn't ever want to go to Mexico. I could use the company."

Jose was not only an employee at the processing plant where we both worked, but he also was a good friend. He was the head honcho of our division of our food processing union and was in touch with what was going on with many employees, including me. "Isn't your wife from Mexico?" I asked, thinking that a person always wanted to go home.

"Yeah, but life wasn't good for her there and she doesn't want to be reminded; she won't go back home."

Our conversation turned back to my being able to go; it seemed he didn't want to talk about his wife's past either. My having a lot of vacation time gave Jose a lot of leverage to convince me. Jose and I became friends through building the union to a strong enough membership to have some negotiating power. I never needed the union for my own benefit but got involved when Jose started pointing out what the company was doing to the immigrant workers from Asia, Central America, and South America, who didn't know their rights—rights they hadn't had in their old countries and so hadn't understood that they now had them, here in the land of opportunity. If those rights weren't used, it was only the land of opportunity to those who exploited them. I resisted this involvement for a long time; saying that I just wanted to take care of my family, but when my marriage fell apart, that changed that viewpoint also.

I was one of those employees who never missed work and even got perfect-attendance certificates at the end of each year. The certificates weren't good for anything; it was just some paper to fill a box of odds and ends that I felt obligated to keep. I got them every year not through effort but through my natural work ethic. Seems like I have always worked, from the time I was able to walk steadily on my feet. When I was little, there were chickens or rabbits to feed, and then with a few more inches of height, there were bucket calves to feed, baby pigs to keep up with, or something else to do—there was never a lack of chores. My father's expectations of me had turned into a way of life; I liked to work and was glad to have it.

I readily agreed with a tall, rugged-looking man with whom I worked, years earlier. He struggled with heavy alcohol use, and he would say, with seriousness and a look of preoccupation, "I have always found hard work to be a cure for many things." But then, sometimes life would become too much for him, and he wouldn't leave his motel room for two or three weeks at a time. When I would call him, his speech was slurred badly, even though he seemingly had his head together. He had an effect on me, and I worked harder, knowing that work was always helping me to get through the heavy issues in life.

However, I was really glad that the perfect-attendance certificates weren't given out in a ceremony, with my coworkers watching. I can imagine how they would call me a "brown nose" or something close to that but maybe not so kind. I didn't go to work every day because I wanted to please the company; it was something that was inside of me. Yet this natural desire to work became an asset when I was put to work on a work crew with eighteen men from the state of Zacatecas, Mexico. At first, they tolerated me at best and poked fun at me, since it was obvious that I knew nothing of beef processing on a fast-pace line, how to keep my knife sharp, or how to speak Spanish—other than taco, burrito, and enchilada.

I did learn that beef tripe was edible when I asked what was in this *menudo* soup I had purchased in the company cafeteria. The ladies knew only enough English to give me what I asked for and take my money. I agreed that the soup was good; especially the spiciness of the soup was savory, but after understanding that *menudo* was beef stomach lining, it took a long time before I sanely asked for another bowl. Then, after I had worked with these hard-working men for several months, they surrounded me at the end of our lunch half-hour while we were waiting for the chain to start its revolutions. The men just looked at me, and I said, "What?" and faced them down. Then, one of the men, who was bilingual, spoke up. "What are you doing here?"

"Why? I'm working."

"Only Mexicans work here for more than two weeks; the work is too hard for white or black men."

I had a beautiful wife at home and a toddler son and a little girl who thought I was something special, and I was determined to take care of them. I told the men that I had a family, and this was the work that I could find, and I couldn't be chased away with a big stick. They seemed satisfied with my answer and accepted me in their group. I was then invited to their private parties and functions. They taught me how to keep my knife razor sharp, so I wouldn't be so fatigued at the end of the day. This work was the hardest work I had ever performed—tougher than the hot-tar roofing crew I had worked on not long after I left home at seventeen.

Narcisco, who stood next to me on the chuck boning line and with whom I worked elbow-to-elbow, started teaching me the phrases and the names of things, helping me to communicate with my coworkers in their own language. He would point at something, like the conveyor belt, and say its name. He would then use the butt of his knife to write out the word in the fat smeared on the white cutting table, where, as the day progressed, we continually flipped and slid the beef chucks. Hence, there was a nice layer of fat on the table all day long to use as a temporary writing tablet—a fatty Etch-a-Sketch. This was the first time in my life that I felt truly accepted by my peers. They saw that there were times when I went to work when I needed to run to the bathroom often, with my guts about to release, or when I was burning up with a fever and could hardly think. My share of the work, however, was always done, no matter how I felt, and they respected me for it. This was just the way I was wired; I went to work every day.

I had just finished the last court date, completing the divorce from the woman to whom I had hoped to be married for the rest of my life. She was with a man she thought was better than me. I just couldn't get her to see that being married fifty-plus years would be a wonderful thing. I felt robbed of my future fiftieth wedding anniversary and the years of waking up every morning with all I ever wanted in my arms. I knew I wasn't the best man, but I was not the worst man either, with a lot to learn. Still, I found myself single again after ten years and emotionally exhausted. I had no idea how to be single and was trying to work things out within my own dripping heart.

Therefore, a trip of nine days—to a place I knew nothing about and where I would understand very little of what was said—appealed to me. My own thoughts needed this time of nothingness. The Spanish I had learned to speak with coworkers wasn't conversational Spanish or words or phrases that could be used outside of the workplace. If truth be said, most of what I understood or could speak wasn't used in polite society. The first two things a person learns in a second language are how to count and how to swear.

It was decided we would take my old four-door 1967 Chevy because it was known that a person shouldn't look like he had much money when he ventures across this southern border. Every official wanted to be bribed and often asked for money, seeming little better than a beggar. If an officer pulled a car over or one was unlucky enough to be stopped at a roadblock, the conversation most often climaxed with a request for dollars. The poorer one could look, the lower the financial request tended to be. Therefore, Jose and I both were dressed in jeans, plain button-up shirts, and cowboy boots, which, I was told, would blend in wherever we went, once across the Mexican-American line. My car didn't look like much, with its unglamorous faded green color. Rust on the rear quarter panels gave it the poor-man look, but it ran well and everything worked, especially the air conditioner, which was very important, as temperatures could reach 108 degrees in northern Mexico.

Outside of Jose's country home, which had roosters crowing out by the chicken coops, tranquility filled the evening. I felt the peace of the setting sun as it neared the western hills, although the huge ball of fire couldn't be seen through the elm trees. I sat on the hood of my car in the shade. I waited while Jose said good-bye to his wife and gave her one last kiss and an embrace. He then got in the passenger side, while I jumped off the hood and waved to his señora, who always smiled nicely at me. I lightly gripped the skinny rim of the steering wheel and pulled out onto the sand road that would lead us to the highway south. We had worked a full day at the plant, but as we were in our early thirties, we never thought of rest or exhaustion. Our plan was to drive all night long and into the next day, until we reached our destination. Every time the gas tank needed refilling, we planned to get some sandwiches or munchies and change drivers, so as too not lose any time.

Jose's hometown was in the mountains of Zacatecas, and I wondered what it would look like and how the people would treat us. He said it was a beautiful place, and he wished he could live there, but there was no work. As close friends, we had talked a lot and knew each other well. Jose knew about my marriage struggles and how I would rather not be single, and I knew that he lived in poverty until he was fifteen, when his father took his family to live in Los Angeles, and why he made a move with his wife and children to the Midwest. It seems that there was just too much violence in that California city in which his family lived. Jose hadn't even known where he was taking his family when he started out on this journey. Once he had made the decision to leave, he loaded up his family and what possessions were important in his huge late-seventies station wagon and a two-wheel trailer made from an old pickup truck box and frame, and they headed out

He would drive east until he found a town that looked decent and where he thought he could get a job. It was time for him and his family to start over. Then, after he had driven for several days, he had stopped to get gas for his car, and he asked the convenience store employee if a man could get a job in that town. The lady motioned toward the plant where I already was an employee and said, "The plant is always hiring."

Jose came to work at the plant and began cutting meat on a revolving chain in the area where I had become a lead man for ten cents more an hour. The lead-man job was just a relief from the hard physical labor of working on the line. I was glad to meet Jose, especially because soon after he and I became friends, my life fell apart, and in many ways, he was support. For Jose, after relocating, his life just got better and better. He had a good home and income, and he got along with his neighbors. By this time his parents had moved back to Mexico and were able to retire.

Before we rolled into Amarillo, Texas, I was falling asleep behind the wheel. Exhaustion had overtaken me, and my alertness was gone. I felt drained by the emotional toll of the love of my life leaving me and the divorce. The judge who had granted us the divorce said that we looked like a nice couple and that we should work it out. He looked frustrated when my wife didn't agree with him. I was losing everything I ever wanted, but my fight was depleted.

Once I was on the road, I became relaxed, and soon Jose was saying, "Pull over; let me drive." Amarillo had been my driving goal. "It's okay. I'm not sleepy." Jose's tone resonated with understanding, and I pulled over on the Texas shoulder.

I awoke again as the car's tires changed tone as Jose left the highway and pulled into a convenience store, somewhere on the edge of Amarillo. I pushed myself hard up out of my slumber and attempted to be alert. I filled up the car up with regular gas, hoping that the cool night air would help me to wake up, while Jose bought fresh cups of coffee, chips, and candy bars. Bugs circled the lights under the canopy above me, and I thought it all was surreal. It was like falling into another world—I'd awakened from my weird dreams to find myself in places without known landmarks. I needed another world.

The old Chevy steered easily with one hand, with the large steering wheel and power-steering accessory. With a disposable cup of coffee in my left hand and my right hand on the steering wheel, we were on the road again. We drove through the night under the dark of the new moon. The car went up and down with the hills and back and forth with the curves along creeks and around large hills. The highway seemed endless, and my head was heavy. The coffee wasn't doing its job. My stare became lower and lower, until I heard Jose's request to drive again. His eyes were bright, and I envied his alertness. I felt sorry that I wasn't able to hold up my end of the bargain and drive a tank full. But his eyes were not condemning, and I consented without resistance because I could use a good nap. It was like I had left all my worries behind, like I had a perfect life—until the dreams came.

I dreamed of my wife, with her long, straight, heavy auburn hair, blue-hazel eyes, and the way she would look at me with tilted head and feminine square jawline. I was content when she looked at me in such a way, but it was a contentment that she didn't share. It didn't make any difference if she was loving or angry at me; I loved being in her presence. She was the only woman I wanted. I looked at other women as being strange and not worth the effort to get to know. I liked the consistency of daily life with her, and work was easy when I was building something for her. I worked for our life and thought life would get better as I learned how to be a better man. I was content with the way she was, with the exception of her discontentment, and I dreamed of her in my emotional distress.

Then I was awakened again by the car slowing and pulling into another late-night convenience store, somewhere in West Texas, where the lady behind the cash register talked about being careful because the deer were running across the highway. She had known a man, who had a deer go through his windshield, and he wasn't sharing life with us anymore.

I wanted to take my turn at driving, but Jose said he was good and he said something about me finally relaxing. I reached for my car keys; but Jose got in under the steering wheel leaving me no choice other than to get in the passenger side. I fell asleep almost as soon as I leaned back in the wide, flat seat, where my wife had sat many times.

In Eagle Pass, where we planned on crossing the border, I woke up again, and the car was stopped. Jose had angle parked on a street with storefronts looming up in front of me in the early morning sun. The sun's glow was lighting the sky from behind the buildings behind us. These businesses, which hadn't yet opened for the day, had colorful displays, and everything was written in Spanish. Jose explained that this wasn't an all-night border crossing, so we had to wait before we could go on into our neighboring country.

While Jose and I waited, we went through the car to make sure all the contents of my car were safe for the border crossing. The car's registration was in the glove box—we would need this to get the permission papers to take my car far down into Mexico. Much to Jose's displeasure, I had forgotten to bring the title of my car with me, but I had more things to take care of before we left than he did—he had a wife to take care of all the household things. I not only had my house to ready for my absence but also had to take care of all the things a single parent has to do. This was a new juggle for me, and I admit that I wasn't very practiced at it.

I also found a box of .22 caliber rifle shells in the glove box. "Those shells would get us put in jail in Mexico," Jose said, alarmed. As much as it hurt, I wrapped the ammunition in some waste paper so they would not be recognized by someone passing by and threw the shells in a public trashcan on the sidewalk. Ammo wasn't cheap, and it was a waste of money, but better to discard them than to find ourselves in a Mexican jail. We searched the car for anything else that could bring us trouble.

"The gates will be open at 7:00 a.m.," Jose explained, looking at his wristwatch. We then drove around for a while between the old storefronts in the narrow streets of Eagle Pass. We couldn't find anywhere to get breakfast We might have found something to eat if we hadn't been concerned about getting too far from the border gates. Jose thought he could work out the lack-of-car-title thing, so we continued to move forward. Finally, I drove south through Eagle Pass and toward the Mexican border gates and waited in a line that had already formed.

One Mexican guard searched my car, while the officer behind the counter asked several questions about travel plans and route. We got the papers to travel—that was after we placed a twenty-dollar bill underneath our papers because of the missing car title. The official behind the counter was satisfied with our papers and delighted with his share of the American wealth. Then we got in our car and drove south again. A few miles farther into Mexico, we drove out of the Free Zone which is a narrow strip along the border before needing Mexican papers to travel farther. Then, as I drove farther down a narrow paved highway, a police officer standing by his patrol car motioned us over. It didn't look right to me, but Jose told me to pull off the road into the abandoned filling station. It was another official, wanting a twenty-dollar bill. When Jose asked why he was asking for the money, he responded, "It is so little to you. You Americans have too much." Without a reason for the officer to gain the money from us, we didn't give it to him. He was disappointed but wasn't able to stop us from driving on—but I think we paid for that later.

A few miles farther down the road, I could see high mountains rising up ahead and a low-lying dry valley. Jose was not sure about which road we should take. There were no stores or any other businesses where we could stop to ask directions. But two young men were walking down the side of the road, carrying canvas bags.

Jose said, "Pull over, and I will ask them."

The men appeared to be in their late twenties and looked rough— almost a working-man appearance but not quite. They didn't seem trustworthy to me. "Are you sure?" I asked Jose.

"They are from here and will know the roads. It'll be okay."

We got our directions from the men, with more conversation about the area and where the roads led. They were pleasant enough. In the process, the young men asked for a ride, and Jose gave them permission to get into the backseat of my '67, but we didn't take our eyes off them. Jose turned in the front passenger seat and watched one, and I watched the other in my rearview mirror. It was self-preservation—we kind of liked life and were both determined to live life as long as possible, and one never knew how desperate another person might be. We dropped them off at the end of a road leading to a manufacturing plant that was about a mile down a thin paved road. The men had told us that this was where they were going to buy rat-poison in bulk. They would repackage it into small packages and sell it on the streets. They had brought their own burlap sacks to carry the questionable substance.

My body relaxed when they were out of my car and walking to the south of the main highway. They were probably just as curious about us as we were about them. It was then that Jose spoke my thought. "Thank you, Lord, for the EPA. Things are different in Mexico. They don't regulate like they do back home."

"They could die from handling the poison," I said, and Jose nodded as he stared down the road. Jose had a heart for the people, which is why he promoted the union.

We found the right road—a thin wavy line—that led across the dry plains toward the mountains. We were on our way farther south, and since the sun up, so was I. Fatigue was no longer a problem, since I'd slept well last night while the tires hummed. I was interested in this land; it was so foreign to me. It was barren of vegetation, and I wondered how anyone lived in such a place.

Jose called my attention to a trail alongside the main highway. "That's a donkey trail."

I soon understood what he meant when I saw a two-wheeled cart, like out of Pancho Villa days, pulled by a donkey. The man on the front of the cart was dressed in homespun clothes, and a blanket, decorated like a Mexican poncho, covered the load. He wore a hat that I wouldn't have called a sombrero in its tattered and smaller form and without any decoration, but that is what I learned the Mexicans called such a hat. Its function was to keep the sun off his face and shield his eyes. I saw many of these carts while in Mexico, among the trucks and cars in the small city's streets or on the donkey trails.

The mountains looked like huge, dry, rocky hills at first, and then we climbed up and up. The mountains held mountains behind mountains and grew in size but their dryness didn't change—a tree was unusual; the cactus wasn't unusual. We drove, taking turns for what seemed to be forever, and intermittently, we came to a flat desert in between the mountains. Surprisingly, at a crossroad in the middle of a desert close to Saltillo, there were some nice shade trees. The federal police under the shade trees, however, weren't so nice.

The police were able to see us coming from afar on the flat, straight highway. We watched while they drove their cars across the highways in every direction as we approached the intersection. They had guns on their hips and rifles in hand. It was a sight for this country boy as they stood facing us between their black cars. I pulled over under the wonderful shade trees, where one of them motioned with a pointing finger. It seemed to me that these armed officers didn't want to stand in the hot sun any more than we did. We got out of the car, and they began to question us. I understood little that was said but had no problem understanding the officer who found my cheap carnival handcuffs hanging under the dashboard, He said to me, *"Éstos son ilegales."* I did have enough sense (or Spanish) to say, *"Es tuyos,"* which means roughly that he could have them. It seemed like the sensible thing—to give this leering officer of the Mexican law ownership of a toy I had won at a carnival and that he said was illegal. I especially thought it was the most sensible thing to say to this Mexican officer when soon we were on the road again—that is, we were on the road again as soon as they had the toy handcuffs and some American cash in their pockets.

With the threat of arrest over and in the rearview mirror, we were gladly on the road again. Soon, we needed fuel, and we pulled into a filling station that was much like the filling stations in the United States before convenience stores became the norm—but not as nice or as clean as I remembered them. There were a couple of dirty gas pumps under a canopy in front of a glassed-in cashier area—with bars over the windows. Two bays, where cars could be worked on, were off to the side of the lobby, but the rollup bay doors were closed.

A group of children came around the corner, clean but in tattered clothing and barefoot, asking for change, which Jose and I obliged. Then a little girl of no more than six years old saw an ink pen through the open door of my car. She asked for it, and I didn't see a problem with giving it to her. As kids are, when her companions saw she had a pen, they wanted one also. Jose and I searched the car for lost pens and pencils—in the glove box, under the front seat, and behind the cushions of the backseat—until each of them had one. My kids had ridden in this backseat for many miles, and there were plenty of forgotten items behind it. And yes, there was enough for all.

I had never seen such poor children and was astonished at what they valued so highly. When the fuel tank was full, the attendant was there to return the hose and nozzle to its place on the pump. He gave us a price, and I, not understanding the Mexican currency or their ways, reached for some money.

Jose leaned around him to check the pump and said, "*No es el precio,*" meaning "That isn't the right price." Jose then mentioned an amount, and the attendant quickly agreed. I paid the correct price, giving the man a bill larger than the price, and he returned the change in pesos to me.

After we were on the road, Jose said, "They will do that down here. They will stand in front of the pump so you can't see the amount and then tell you a higher price. I can't stand a thief." I then understood that Jose had kept a watch on the pump's rotating numbers, so that when the attendant moved to hide the numbers, he would already know what we owed. I wondered if the pump even pumped the full amount of fuel that registered on its dial, but I could do nothing about that kind of dishonesty, so I let the thought go. My car didn't have the same power on this fuel as on US fuel, but it ran, and I was glad to be moving down the road between the mountains and Joshua trees.

The mountains peaks with their high passages came up steep as we drove to surprising heights. Then the road dropped off steep but not as far down as we had traveled up. We drove across more long, flat, cactus-covered plains, stretching far between mountains and up and down steep grades on straight highways that were awfully narrow when compared to US highways. The slim pavement was stressful and made me think the approaching cars may smack our fenders but that never happened.

We found ourselves behind a heavily loaded semi-truck, creeping slowly up a grade. At the top of the grade, I whipped around the truck and flew past him. Soon, I exclaimed, "What the heck!"—the truck was on my tail, with its huge pipe bumper and grill guard filling all my rearview mirrors.

Jose said, "Get moving! He will push you off the road if you are in his way." The truck had been down to 10 or 15 mph on the upgrade, but now, on the downgrade, he was up to 80 or 90 mph. The edge of the pavement dropped off to rough, steep, sloped rocky ditches. "They overload the trucks here," Jose commented, "and no one weighs the trucks."

I was glad for the next upgrade to make some distance between the truck and me, while the trucker struggled to climb another grade. I never got in front of another semi-truck. We drove on uneventfully for hours, feeling like we were in the Twilight Zone. We reached a point where Jose and I both stopped talking altogether, and we just listened to the best radio station we could find. I had never driven this far in one stretch, so this was broadening my mind and settling my heart. When the transmission of one radio station would become too overridden with static, we rolled the tuning knob back and forth until we found another station that brought in clearly some sort of Mexican music and a jabbering DJ. We sometimes turned off the radio when no stations came in clearly. The wind passed the open windows, and we watched the passing desert. Here, the desert full of Joshua trees grew in every direction. The trees had a spooky appearance in the dimming twilight.

Jose said, "The branches of those trees look like the deformed arms of the overworked packing-house workers, like they have been worked until they are crippled."

At that point, the trees took on a different appearance to me, and I felt sadness—Jose and I both new these people. The realization that some people only had laborious work in their future brought the Burl Ives version of the song "Sixteen Tons" streaming through my mind. I then thought that even the precious work could be taken away by uncaring people who pushed them to a point of permanent injury.

The cloudless blue sky was full in the windshield as the old Chevy topped the mountain ridge. Then the pale-green hood in front of the windshield dipped down over its edge toward Monte Escobedo, Zacatecas, which spread out wide from mountain range to mountain range. The buildings seemed to go on endlessly. Toward the city's center, business buildings stood tall, like the hub of a wagon wheel with low-lying houses filling the space in the surrounding foothills. All the houses and buildings were of concrete or stone. I loved the sight, looking down from the heights. Once inside the city, I found my estimation of the building materials to be generally true. We stopped at a local car mechanic's garage, at Jose's request and direction. It seemed to be in the central part of the town. I drank some real Coke out of the tall, returnable bottles. The Coke fizzled up my nose, as it had in my youth. I watched and listened while obvious friends caught up with each other, although I could only listen to the rhythm of the words and sentences. The words rattled between men sitting on buckets and whatever else would serve the purpose. I could see that Jose was home. We left the working men after their courteous "Mucho gusto" and salutations.

I followed Jose's instructions—he'd said he wanted to see something—turning here and turning there, until we drove down a street where a construction site progressed below us. Jose stretched up and said, "There he is." He pointed at a redheaded young man with a reddish complexion, working with a shovel in his hand. Perplexed, I responded, "Well he's working."

"But he works as a laborer"

"At least he has a job and wants to work."

Jose said, "He takes jobs away from Mexicans who need jobs, and he's doing what any man can do. Why doesn't he go back to the USA, where he came from? Jobs are plentiful up there."

The sun was now nearing the western mountain range. We found the highway leading south of Monte Escobedo. The highway grew dark in the shadow of the mountains as I turned off onto a narrower paved road. This road led straight to the mountainside that seemed to go up forever at an alarming rate, and there was no visible passage. The mountains were black as the sun set behind them. The high peaks could barely be seen against the dark, moonless sky. Somewhere in the foothills, we turned north, parallel with the line of mountains, and we steadily rose in altitude. Once we were up on the mountainside, the road switched back south. The highway switched back and forth as the valley darkened, and the sun's glow vanished. We continued farther north and then rounded the mountain where it jutted out.

On a flat area outside the curve were two cars with dented fenders, and bloody bodies were lying on the road's edge. Red lights were flashing too brightly. I slowed to make sure that I stayed on the road and didn't hit anything, which wasn't too easily done with all the shimmering lights. Jose had been half sleeping in the passenger seat—it had been a long day and a half—but then, alarmed, Jose shot straight into alertness. "Don't stop! They rob people that way!"

I had no intention of stopping, but also I did not desire to go over the mountainside or hit any car that might be coming around the obscured curve. I continued as fast as I thought was safe to do so. Meanwhile, Jose was locking the doors. Once we were past the car wreck, everything turned dark again, except for the headlight-illuminated section of the road ahead and the mountainside. One side was always rocks and mountainside, and the other was as black as an antique hearse. There was no end to the darkness on the valley side.

The road turned to gravel. Jose said, "They were paving our road to the town and then suddenly stopped."

"Why?"

"The money ran out before they were done. The money allocated for the highway just disappeared." I couldn't see Jose, as I was concentrating on the road, but he seemed to be staring straight ahead. He added, "It was the same with our school. You will see it. The school only has walls, and that is where they stopped building. Now, cactus grows inside the walls."

"What happened to the money?"

"There is a lot of corruption, and one can never get answers." Jose sounded very serious, so I left it alone.

We rose up to the crest of the ridge. Rocks and pine trees were on both sides of the narrow gravel road, and then the road narrowed even more. The trees and rocks along the roadside were now gone. "Wow, its dark on both sides of the road," I commented.

Jose was sitting straight up. "Don't swerve off the road. We are on a ridge, and it is miles down on either side. Just be careful."

I was as alert as a paranoid outlaw, holed up in a motel room, and I sat up so straight that I'm sure that my back wasn't touching the back of the seat. I wished Jose was driving, but then, I also wanted to be in control at this point. Which option was better, I didn't know.

My back and neck muscles didn't relax until the road widened a little, and then, a little farther along, there was vegetation on both sides of the road. We were then on a mountain mesa. We drove across the mesa, straight north, for miles, and the rock road was flat. The road turned east and was rocky, with washboard grooves cut through it at times, but the same fairly flat and straight road. The road dipped a little, and as we approached a low narrow bridge, a vehicle came from the other side with its bright headlights on. I was concerned because the road was so narrow, and I was no longer able to see the bridge banisters as we drove over the small ravine. I flashed the approaching vehicle with my bright headlights, but Jose immediately yelled, "No!"

Then off-road lights came on across the top of the truck facing us. I could see only the bug splatters glaring across my windshield. The hood of my old car was imperceptible. I slammed on the brakes. The front end of my car slid sideways to a stop.

"Stay in the car," Jose said as he jumped out. He disappeared past the searchlight brightness. After a few minutes, the bright road lights went out, and he returned to the car, and the headlights dimmed. My eyes took a minute to adjust to where I could see anything. "Don't flash your bright lights at anybody down here," Jose instructed. "That family runs this area, and we don't mess with them. They will kill you, and no one will be able to do anything about it."

That was a lesson learned, and I still don't flash my bright headlights at people to this day.

It was the season for the fall festivals, and every village had one in progress. We saw a lot of colored lights and people milling around in the streets as we passed through towns. When the Laguna Grande's lights were few miles ahead, we stopped off where there was a dance as part of this fall festival. I could see from a distance that Laguna Grande was a *pueblito* (a small town or village). It was Friday night, and the dance had just started, even though it was late. I was to understand later that in the Mexican culture, the dances started at about ten in the evening and ran until three in the morning. The dance hall overwhelmed me with the volume of the band echoing off the adobe walls under a metal roof. There were no acoustics or anything to buffer the band's blast. Evidently, the building was normally used to shelter farm equipment, but it was now swept clean, and tables and chairs lined the sides, with the exception of the bandstand at the center of the back wall. There was also a beer bar in the corner to the right of the huge sliding doors as we walked in. The bar was simple. Four fifty-five gallon oil drums with two-by-twelve wood boards across their tops created a bar and separated the customers from the several bartenders. Against the wall behind the makeshift bar was an oblong galvanized livestock watering tank, filled with ice and several brands of beer. This was not unlike some country dances or parties I had attended in the Midwest. *Tamborazo*[2] music echoed off the walls, with its heavy drumbeat. The sound was deafening until one had a chance to soak up a few *cervezas*, which took the edge off the boom-boom effect of the drums.

I was introduced to some of Jose's cousins when they came to greet him. I'd always found it interesting that Jose seemed to never sit down, and this situation was no different. He stood and introduced me, and then, in his assertive way, Jose excused himself, saying he had things to do. His cousins and I sat at a large round table. They were gracious and accepted me into their circle. I found it to be a nice, relaxing time. I felt at home. My new friends kept buying Tecates (a type of beer) and putting one in front of me. I can't say that I resisted very much. Of course it wouldn't have been polite for me not to buy a round after they each had bought one. It was amazing how much better my Spanish became after a few *cervazas* had built me up, yet I had no idea how to ask for beer in their language. There were no customers at the bar when I stood up to go for my round, only bartenders. One leaned back against the galvanized beer cooler, and the other two leaned against the wood planks and visited with a lady who kept their attention. This was daunting, but I persisted.

I took my time, until there was another man at the counter purchasing beer. I stepped up behind him, and the two bartenders who weren't busy just glanced at me and went back to their conversation with the pretty lady. I heard the man in line ahead of me say, "*Quiero dos Coronas, por favor.*" The man delivered the two bottles of Corona and asked for four thousand pesos. The transaction was completed quickly, and the customer in a black cowboy hat and western dress turned and walked away.

I said almost the same phrase to the bartender, except I asked for Tecates. "*Quiero cinco Tecates, por favor.*" It was an easy step for me to repeat what the other man had said, substituting the number of and brand of beer. The bartender brought the five beers and asked for ten thousand pesos. I handed him a twenty-thousand–peso paper bill, and he gave me

---

2   A regional music named after a drum, which is a centerpiece for the band.

the correct change. *Life is good*, I thought and smiled at my success in my first purchase in Mexico. I felt like I could be a Mexican entrepreneur. I handed out the beers to my new friends and felt good, inside and out..

It was a good evening. I learned to speak more Spanish, made new friends, heard a genre of music that I had never heard, and made many successful purchases—I bought every fifth round all night long—in a new language in a new country. I was careful to keep my wits; I was in a strange place, and Jose did not return until the band was saying *buenas noches* and was packing up their instruments. Jose seemed a little tipsy to me when he walked in the dance hall. He told me that he would drive, and because I was tired, I didn't argue. I just tossed the keys to him, and we slid into the car. Jose drove while I watched the fascinating pueblo as we approached then observed everything as we drove in between its buildings.

The only law enforcement was the overly armed officer at the dance, in work shirt and rough-spun pants. His clothes caused him to appear to be from an older world than we lived in. He stood at the side of the dance, first in one place and then another, a big handgun on his side and a rifle in his hands as he kept watch on everyone. His armaments trumped those of the federal police with whom we previously had come into contact— he had belts of bullets across his chest. He looked like someone out of Poncho Villa movies. This was something I thought I would never see. I humorously thought that if he didn't get us with his pistol, he would with his rifle, if he had the mind to. He definitely wouldn't run out of bullets, even his gun belt had loops filled with ammo.

As we drove through town, I noticed that Jose was drunker than I'd thought. Yet I wasn't worried since this was Jose's hometown, and he knew where we were going. We drove all over the pueblito of stone buildings and cobblestone streets. Jose pointed out buildings and talked about them. It had rained lightly, and because the cobblestones were worn smooth, the streets became slick. Jose was driving slowly, so the slick streets shouldn't have been a problem, but a large stone stood up out of the street at a street corner. Jose turned too short and the stone, which was about three feet high, struck the rear driver's side door, causing the car to stop. When Jose pressed down on the gas pedal, the back tires began to spin on the wet stones. Jose continued to press down on the gas pedal, and the tires continued to spin with a whine. Jose had his eyes focused to somewhere out the windshield. I was laughing because it was obvious that he thought he was going forward. "Jose! Jose!"

"What?"

"You're up against a rock."

Jose slurred, "What rock?"

"It's up against the back door," I said. "Look out your window."

Jose looked out the window, and after shifting up and down on the stick shift, he found the reverse gear, backed up the car, and then promptly pulled the gear shift into the drive gear … and hit the rock again. Tires squalled on the damp cobblestone—again. Once again Jose looked forward to where he thought he was going.

"Jose! Jose!" I hollered over the music on the AM station, a Spanish version of a love-gone-wrong song.

"What?"

"You are up against the rock again."

Jose looked out the window and backed the car up again. He started to pull forward without steering around the obstacle. I reached over and turned the steering wheel so he could get around the stone. Jose came to his senses and stopped the car, got out, and looked at the scrape on my car. He apologized several times. I wasn't worried about the car; it was still functional, and it had never been pretty or classy.

We toured the town several times over while we drank more beer from a carton on the bench seat between us—Jose had gotten it somewhere. The town was small and resembled something out of a Clint Eastwood western movie. It was quiet and peaceful, and the rain had stopped, leaving a glimmer quality. It was a pleasant place to be.

Jose's parents were up when we arrived at their house, which was an old Spanish monastery. It was after midnight, and they opened the eighth of an inch–thick steel door that come together in two halves, from top to bottom, after recognizing their son's voice. The doors were two narrow doors over the top of the original hand-carved wood door of the house. The steel-plate door could only be opened from the inside of the house. Light shone through the door out into the dimly lit street where we stood, and Jose's elderly father stepped back and let us in, greeting us in the front room. Moments later, Jose's mother entered. Jose introduced me and explained to them that I spoke and understood very little Spanish.

His parents were gracious and polite. This low-lit room had an ornate ceramic floor and plaster walls—at this point that was all I saw. It struck me as Jose's parents greeted us that there were no hugs or noticeable excitement about their son's coming home. I knew it had been a year since they'd last seen each other. I could see there was love, just not displayed. Our conversation was short, as we were tired from a long drive and partying, and Jose showed me a room with a bed.

When I awoke the next morning, the sun was bright and shining through the curtain laced window. When I fully arose and sat on the edge of my bed, I could see the softened light coming in from an inner patio through an overhead lattice. The sun was obscured behind the east part of the stone house. I was soon to discover that Jose was gone, and only his mother was home. I was in dire need of a restroom and went to look for it. I found it, after passing through another bedroom. It contained an old wardrobe against one wall, with a bed sitting in the middle of the far wall, but that was all the furnishings. There wasn't even a picture or painting on the wall. I found a room without a door, where I could see a sink in a simple vanity, with an old Spanish-style framed mirror above it. I ventured farther into the room and saw an opening with a commode against the wall.

I felt odd using a commode in a room without a door. I very much wanted to close a door. Afterward, I noticed a shower, but it was not like I was used to seeing in people's homes; it was much like I had known in my high school—several showerheads were in a white ceramic-tile room.

I looked everything over and noticed another style of wardrobe that most likely served as a storage unit for towels and washcloths. I showered and felt more alive. Then I noticed the ceiling was high. I was looking up at the unusual ceiling when Jose's mother came walking by. She greeted me and asked, in her best English, if I was hungry. When I said I was, she fed me baked chicken and eggs for breakfast. (Jose told me on the return trip that she didn't know what I liked to eat so she fed me what she had.)

In the daylight, I was able to look over the house. I had never seen a home in its old Spanish style. The house was built in a squared-off horseshoe shape, with a wall across the back. The back wall had a large wooden door in the middle of it, and the door led to a second patio, where the livestock was kept at night. The livestock always wandered in just before sunset and always found a secure bed for the night, and then the door was closed. On the road trip, Jose had explained that his parents had bought the old monastery years ago before they moved back to their hometown. They had repaired and remodeled the old building. It still had the hard-packed clay roof, with just enough slope for the rain to run off during early springtime—the rainy season. The outside walls were about five feet thick at the bottom and leaned inward, while the interior was straight up, to a height of approximately twenty feet. The ceiling on the inside of the house was about eighteen feet high and was made of rough cedar. Every five feet or so there were rough cedar poles extending from the inside patio walls to the outside walls. This house appeared to be out of the old western movies or history books and was thought to be the oldest building on the mesa. The clay roof was supported by ax-split wood laid over the top of the poles. The sun had baked the clay hard, into a pale yellow solid surface that insulated the home and shed rainwater. The roof was effective and lent its charm to the décor on the inside of the house.

When Jose's parents had bought the house, it had clay floors throughout, but those were hard to keep clean and level, so they had replaced the clay with concrete floors in every room and then laid ceramic tile over it, giving it an elegant, pleasing atmosphere that one just wanted to languish in. There were huge windows for viewing and ventilation into the inner patio. I spent some time walking around in the house and observed that there were few things hanging on the walls or sitting on the sparse furniture. It was kept simple but somehow relaxing and rich. I walked onto the patio to find a huge grapevine, the base of which was at least six inches thick, growing up to a trellis about nine feet overhead, providing shade. Beauty and antiquity blended in such a way that coziness was the rule.

At this point, my loss back home didn't exist. I had to appreciate the sandstone and everything else that was used to build the house, and I wondered how far the stone and timber had been hauled. I thought about the laboring hands and backs that had built this former monastery. The interior plaster was painted with skill. The house had an appeal like I had never seen.

I ate the chicken with dark baked skin that had a pleasant, unusual flavor, as well as the fried eggs Jose's mother placed in front of me. She sat straight-backed in a chair across the dining table as I ate. She was very gracious in keeping my plate full until I said, *"Ya no, por favor"* ("No more, please"), but even so, she appeared to be uncomfortable in my presence. I reflected on the fact that she and I were the only people in the house, and she might be uncomfortable with being alone with a man or a stranger.

I decided to explore the town and the celebration. As I came out of the house and looked back at it, I was stirred by the sight. I had not expected to see such beauty—the exterior of the house was spectacular, with its native stone in natural shapes cemented together. Small windows were high up, with bars over small square panes of stained glass. The old monastery was the last house on the street running along the natural lake. From there, a sparse cornfield stretched out to the edge of the *laguna*. Past the field, I expected to see mountains. I explored all around town but didn't see any mountains. This was surprising, after driving through mountains and up mountains the evening before to get to this mesa. Looking all around, there were only a few peaks visible southeast of the mesa, and those peaks could barely be seen; I wondered at it and realized the altitude I was in—I felt on top of the world and speculated about all who lived here on top of the world continually. It was wonderful to live in a place where the outside world mattered little. There were no TV stations and no freeways or even a paved road. Tranquil was the way the town felt; nothing else existed but this simplicity.

Music drifted to my ears as I walked toward the town's square. Remembering last night's closed-up festival booths, I walked in that direction. I saw water glimmering blue a short way down a street to the south. I wanted to see everything and turned to walk in that direction. The buildings went down to the water's edge, and the street's stones extended into the little lake. No boats were on the lake, but a few rowboats were pulled up on the east bank. Ducks swam without noticing me or anything else.

I realized the mesa was almost flat; it sloped down to the lake all the way around, so there was enough runoff to create the prettiest little lake. The town lay along the north side of the lake's edge. The tassels of the corn were full and brown, while the cornstalks were all bright green. The blue of the lake, green cornfields, and a sandstone town with the twin towers of the Catholic Church rising above it made a Picasso painting uninviting by comparison.

I turned back toward the center of town after taking in this scene. The music came from various places. Some of the music was recorded and blasted out over cheap stereo systems in colorful stands. Live bands, looking for donations, played under shade trees or beneath tarps stretched between structures. A couple of traditional Mexican bands walked behind people who proudly carried pottery glasses in their hands. Everyone was dressed in their finest. The band members wore decorated sombreros and black suits. The people's dress was conservative, with the women in long dresses of native colors or Spanish styles and many men in suits. Others dressed in cowboy boots, blue jeans, and hats. The trees were not very tall around the square, but they provided plenty of shade with their widely spreading branches. The air was pleasant.

Games of all kinds for adults and children lined the town square, and small carnival rides of all sorts were available for the kids. The carnival rides reminded me of those I had ridden as a child. The roller coaster rattled and sounded as if it would fly apart but nevertheless was filled with screaming children. All of them seemed unsafe as it went around its humpy-bumpily track, and I am sure it would have been shut down if it had been in the United States. But no one seemed concerned, and all looked to be having a good time.

Everything was fascinating, and I was enjoying the atmosphere when a BB stung the side of my head. I realized why the only people close to this booth were the participants with BB guns against their shoulders. I had walked in between the observers and the contestants. The competitors were trying to knock bean bags with hand-painted red stars off narrow shelves. There was nothing to keep the BBs from ricocheting out toward the people. I stepped into the crowd as the little mariachi band in a Plexiglas case started playing. A young man chose a large dangling stuffed animal from the awning of the booth. The prize animals were the same as those in the carnivals I knew back home.

Jose walked up while I was watching to see if another bean bag would fall. He held up one of those pottery glasses in his hand and asked, "Have you tried one of these yet?" He asked one of his *compadres* to get me one. Jose watched me closely as I sipped it to see my response. The drink had a lime flavor and fruit pulp that I assumed came from limes. It had a slow sweetness and then the very noticeable alcohol flavor. I didn't ask what was in it, and I still don't know.

I noticed people watching me. It was odd to see everyone observing me, like I was an oddity. I found a clothing store and bought a white cowboy hat like everyone else wore and this reduced the attention I got. Jose showed me where to buy the concoction that put us in a jolly mood. The beverage was great, but I was careful to not get intoxicated. This wasn't my town or country, and I wanted to keep my wits.

Jose and I walked around with some of his friends. It was hard for me to imagine Jose living here as a child because it didn't seem like him. He was college educated and very businesslike. When Jose's friends noticed me watching the bands that followed people about the town square, they explained to me that if a person wanted to hire a band, it would follow that person around to show that he was well off. I thought that was interesting and humorous.

After wandering around, we found ourselves at the rooster fights. It was just like a miniature bullfight ring, with bleachers set up all around the ring. The ring was made of corrugated metal sheets a few feet high. Sand covered the floor. It was a crude and effective circle. After every fight, a ten-year-old boy jumped in with a fine rake and smoothed the sand back while the rhetoric about the last fight and the fight that was ready to begin was blasted over loud speakers. People loved volume in this part of the world, so it seemed.

I saw a stock tank full of ice and beer in a back corner, so I went to it and repeated the same sentence as I had at the dance last night and bought beers for all of us. I was feeling successful. Jose's friends left so that it was only Jose and I at the chicken fights. Before I finished my second beer, Jose left with other friends, but I was glad he was catching up with people he didn't see every day. I would have been no different with my childhood friends, so I enjoyed the fights until I was tired of sitting and was hungry.

There were many rich and wonderful smells coming from the food stands. All of the food looked good, but none of it was anything I associated with traditional Mexican food. Without any reference point, I didn't know how to ask for any food. I waited then saw someone approach a food stand. I stepped right up behind him and listened to how he asked for his food; like a mocking bird I repeated him and had food to eat. It was success

My meal was wrapped in plain brown paper and was very warm, as it had just been cooked in a skillet over a propane burner at the little food stand. The food had flavor in abundance. It was chicken and a blend of vegetables in a tortilla. It was delicious and I had successfully satisfied my hunger.

I bought some things from the booths for keepsakes and gifts for my children by pointing my fingers and saying a phrase I had heard over and over: "*Cuánto es?*" ("How much?") The sun was nearing the horizon as I walked toward Jose's parents' home. I was glad when the door opened when I knocked. Jose was in the living room with his family, and the small fireplace in the corner had a nice fire in it. The evening air had turned chilly, and the warm flames felt good. At this altitude, the midsummer night air could be quite cool.

I mostly listened to the rhythm and the romantic sound of the Spanish language as the family chatted; not wondering what they were saying but sitting in a relaxed, recuperative state of mind and being. I had peace.

We ate a light evening meal of pork and cornmeal, and then Jose and I decided to go to the Saturday night dance. When I couldn't find my jacket, I mentioned it to Jose, who asked his mother about it. She had hung it on a wooden hanger in the wardrobe.

We got the car out of the garage to drive to the dance—Jose's father thought it best that we keep my car in the garage after the incident with the headlights on the way in town. He knew that association could bring trouble to his door if my car was in front of his house, yet we didn't have any problems, by the Lord's blessings.

At the dance I saw one of Jose's female cousins—I'd admired her the evening before. She carried herself with a confidence that was hard for me to understand. She seemed gentle and intuitive. She also walked with grace. Rachela looked at me steadily with her dark brown eyes. I liked these aspects of her, but my divorce had left me unsure about the romantic side of my life, and I was reluctant to step out. I ignored Rachela's steady looks that stopped someplace behind the optic nerve of my eyes. I got up and moved around the dance hall, avoiding her brown eyes.

I wanted to dance to this new-to-me music. The music had a nice dance beat, and there were many on the dance floor. I approached a lady close to my age who was sitting at a table. I said, "*Danza con mi?*" and she said something I didn't understand—but I did understand that it was a no. I asked several other ladies without success. There were men here who worked at the same plant where Jose and I worked. I recognized several faces, and I approached a man I knew. We talked a short while, and then I said, "I love this music and would like to try to dance to it, but none of the ladies will dance with me."

"What are you saying to them," he asked.

"*Danza con mi,*" I said, which made no sense in any language.

My friend chuckled. "Ask permission this way: *Quieres bailar conmigo?* Anyway," my friend continued, "every woman here has her mother, grandmother, or aunt sitting back watching, and these ladies won't dance with someone they don't know. They mostly only dance with their fiancés or husbands."

I laughed because I felt better at this explanation, "Then how do I dance to this music?"

"I will ask my cousin, and she will dance with you."

He returned after talking to a woman with flaxen hair, and she did dance with me. What I wasn't prepared for was that she wouldn't look at me throughout the entire dance, and there was at least four inches between us at all times—at her insistence, which wasn't said in words, but I understood her gentle firmness. This was all strange to me, but I acknowledged that this was a culture different from my own, and it was to be respected. After the dance, I returned to my table, where Rachela still looked at me with those steady brown eyes. I was trying to ignore her eyes that were so appealing to me, so every so often I'd go for a round of beer, just as a distraction.

My personal peace felt like an unseen substance around me that nothing could penetrate. As the night went on, I didn't understand everything that happened or that was said around me, but sometimes I pretended to understand and just said, "Sí." Yet I had a better idea of what Rachela was saying when she asked, "*Contento?*" That was close enough to English that I assumed she was asking if I was happy, and I responded with a more confident, "Sí."

I was finally feeling the effects of the beer and was relaxed to the point that the loss of my life's love wasn't a thought. I had picked up a few more words in Spanish and was trying to use them. I was becoming comfortable with my surroundings. Jose popped in for a moment to ask how I was getting along, and when he saw that I was comfortable, he said, "I like taking you with me. You are always okay wherever you may be, even when I leave you alone."

"Yes," I agreed, "I am content no matter where I am. I can make the best of it."

I went for another round of beers, but when the bartender set the beer on the wood plank in front of me, he said, "*Veinte mil pesos.*" Twenty thousand? This was twice the amount I had paid previously for the five beers, so I responded, "*No, es diez mil pesos.*" Ten thousand pesos was what I had been paying for the beer.

He laughed and asked, "Where are you from?"

Surprised that he spoke English, I responded, "The Midwest in the United States."

The bartender said, "You have been buying beer from me these last two nights, and I thought you were from here." He laughed heartily, with a gleam in his eye.

"How is it that you speak English so well?" I asked.

"I worked at beef-packing plants in the United States for many years," he answered.

We had a sort of a friendship by this point, so I questioned the price of beer again.

He smiled. "I was just checking to see if you understood."

I said to the still chuckling bartender, "Well, my phrase in Spanish worked the first time, and I find that you don't mess with success."

7

Johnnie Walker

Johnnie Walker didn't drink whisky or any alcohol—not even for his namesake. He was an odd neighbor—maybe old Johnnie could be considered eccentric, but most definitely he was odd. He never went to church, even though he would preach the gospel to anyone if he had the chance. Old Johnnie lived within a mile of our little country church, where he would have been welcomed.

This little church sat on the side of a sand road with its cemetery on the other side, where old Johnnie had been assigned a plot just by the asking. One was supposed to be a member of the First Methodist Church to be buried in their cemetery, so by rights, he shouldn't have gotten this plot, but no one said a word when it was told that Johnnie had asked to be signed up for his little plot of land for the future. It was strange how he could quote the Bible at any time, on any subject, yet no one had ever seen him read the Bible or hear a sermon. This set Johnnie Walker up as a source of jokes in our county but never cruelly. I think that most folks liked him. He was always polite—never verbally rude or insulting—yet he was surly, without aiming his discontent toward any particular person.

We lived in the center of the Midwest in the 1960s. Johnnie's home was not far from the continental center of the United States. The entire world had been using tractors for fifty years or more, but not Johnnie Walker; he farmed with mules. There were no tractors on his eighty acres, just four mules, all with girls' names, even though they were all jacks (male mules). When Johnnie wanted the mules to come in, he would stand up on the wagon and yell out pretty girls' names at the ornery mules. They would come up from their pasture but not too close. They knew their names all right, but they would only come up to about forty feet from him and just look at Johnnie, as if to say, "What do you want?"

The mules just stood there while he cursed at them for stopping short and not coming into the corral, which was the only time he ever cursed. The mules and Johnnie worked together at tilling the land, but they also were at odds with each other. Johnny and the mules were as grouchy as cornered raccoons. It was hard to tell who took on whose personality, but I personally think the mules took on old Johnnie's cantankerousness.

Only once did I get in the corral with the mules. When Alice turned to kick me with both hind hooves, I moved faster than I ever had and still felt a wind off the mule's hooves skim past me. The old jack was huge and muscled from pulling farm equipment. That was when I fully understood why Dad wouldn't get in the corral with the mules and had told me not to do so either. Matter of fact, even Johnnie was mighty cautious when working around the mules.

When I was safely sitting with my dad on the fence rail after Alice tried to kick me, dad looked at me with concern and then laughed hard and slapped me on the back, saying, "You won't be doing that again."

There were only a few occasions when old man Johnnie Walker came over to our farm. He was an amazing sight as he sat with his back straight and away from the backrest of his old Model B Ford pickup truck. He looked determined as he steered the truck into our farmyard. It wasn't originally a pickup truck; it had been a panel wagon when it was new, but somewhere along the line, the body had been cut down and formed into a regular pickup truck cab. A pickup box of about the same year sat on the frame behind the cab, so that at first glance, it looked right—until you saw it was welded together.

The truck was a piece of work, just like its driver. One of those times when Johnnie came over, he complained to Dad that his horn didn't work. Upon inspection, it was determined that there was no positive wire going to the steering column to power the horn button. We had no idea why he needed a horn because no one in that part of the county would blow their horn at someone else; that would have been rude. Maybe Johnnie wanted to honk at the mules, but it really didn't matter. Mr. Walker wanted it to work. Most likely, he wanted conversation and company more than the horn, which he got, because no one in our part of the country got together just to work; it was also to talk and share information about what was going on in the county community.

We were a long way out in the country, and we didn't always have everything we thought we needed, so often, we made something work that was just pure country-boy engineering. Well, Dad noticed that there was a clean shot between the battery positive post on Johnnie's truck and the wire that needed to be hot to make the horn work. He got a piece of baling wire and attached it to the stranded wire that stuck out of the steering column. Then he loosened the nut on the positive battery cable clamp and clamped the wire on tight with the same nut. When the horn button was pressed, the horn honked.

When old man Johnnie saw that, he pushed his cap up and scratched his head where there was still some hair. We most likely could have gone to one of the old cars that sat rusting out in the weeds in an empty lot and found a used piece of automotive electrical wire, but regardless of whether this was the right way to make the repair, when the button was pushed, the horn worked. After more conversation about who was having trouble with a combine harvester or who got how much rain, Johnnie climbed up in his truck, and just as determinedly as he drove in, he drove his aging truck down our driveway to the county road and back to his eighty acres.

A very noticeable aspect of Johnnie Walker was that he wore bib overalls that were light blue and had tiny red and dark blue stripes in the denim. The red stripes in Johnnie's overalls were the indicator of how long it had been since he bathed; the brighter the red stripes the more recent he had bathed but by bathing time the red stripes were unperceivable. When he came to our farm or we went to his, I would always check the wind direction and stand upwind from him. And it was no different on the day he showed up on a hot afternoon, when we were putting new piston rings in the Farmall tractor under a huge, fruitless mulberry tree. I can't remember the conversation that day, but I stood upwind, looking up at the large leaves shining and rustling overhead.

After Johnnie left, I heard Dad say to Mom, "Soon Johnny will be bathing. I couldn't see the red stripes in his overalls." That was the first time I had ever thought to observe those kinds of things. and I was to learn that every time before he bathed, he would go to same clothing store—it was in a town about eleven miles away, which was quite a trip for our thrifty neighbor. This town provided the few things that he ever wanted. At the clothing store—or so it was circulated through the grapevine— he always bought a new pair socks, a flannel shirt, bib overalls, long johns, and a railroad-style cap, which had the same pattern and denim material as his bib overalls, once a year. There were few secrets in our farming community, and this was no different; matter of fact, it was quite a happening. This news always spread quickly among our neighbors, and most folks chuckled and smiled at this fact telling us that Johnnie's bathing time had come. Many were relieved, and all were grateful.

No one ever tried to change him. People were left alone in those days, as long as they weren't hurting anyone, and unquestionably, no one would ever have been rude and said anything to old Johnnie about his odor or appearance. Some of the men said that before Johnnie's brother, Tom, passed away, he was always clean and was more social. Tom and Johnnie would attend most of the area's social functions. Folks saw them on the sidewalks, watching the parade floats go by—they especially admired the antique cars (they remembered when most of the old cars were brand new). They attended the local monthly card parties held in a one-room schoolhouse, turned into a community center in the hills where we lived and where we played ten-point pitch. Tom and Johnnie were partners, and sometimes they would come head-to-head with my father and mother, and it was a battle. Everyone wanted to win, although there was no real prize for winning, except that folks would talk about who was so skilled. Yet a nice piece of apple pie or peach cobbler, after the playing cards were decked and slid into their thin cardboard cases, was always a treat, along with a hot cup of strong coffee to complement the flavor. The chitter-chatter afterwards was as much a prize of the games as were the novel gifts and desserts and coffee, which kept most folks coming in off the hill farms to our the social gatherings. Everyone came as couples, though not necessarily man and wife, and Johnnie Walker's partner was his brother—but now Tom was gone.

I was not yet a preteen at the time that I knew Old Johnnie, and as I carried out my duties and did my assigned chores, I humorously decided that his bathing pattern kept the chores on his farm to a minimum. There wasn't electricity or natural gas in his house. When the old man bathed, extra water had to be carried in from the well, where he watered his mules, and heated on the woodstove. Woodstoves took time in kindling, and whenever a woodstove was used, it meant that wood had to be chopped and split and carried into the house. Much ahead of time, trees must be cut down and chunked up in order for sappy wood to dry, or it wouldn't burn. Chunking of the trees was done with a buzz saw in those days, which was powered by a tractor that Johnnie didn't have. Splitting wood meant swinging an ax. The old man just didn't modernize with the times. Everyone else had moved up to propane heating and cooking stoves. As did many folks who went through the "Dirty Thirties," Johnnie wouldn't spend any more money than he had to. He would find a way to get along with what he had—that was just his way, even if it meant not bathing too often. The local banker would never divulge anyone's financial situation, yet he always solemnly agreed—as he shuffled his feet in the dirt when at a town picnic or such—that Johnnie had ample money to put in a propane water heater and cook stove. He just never joined the people in his age group, who also had lived through those same barren times, who saw the need to live comfortably with such luxuries. But then, if a person only bathes once every year or so, then there was no reason to modernize.

Johnnie's weathered two-story house stood high on a hill at one of the main country crossroads, known then as Johnnie Walker Hill. Most of the countryside's folks traveled past the hill, located where two crushed limestone roads intersected. There were no real trees to speak of on Johnnie's corner, nothing to buffer the cold winter winds or the hot summer gusts and sun. There was only a house, small barn, and a long shed with sliding doors on one side.

He had a dog of so many breeds that no one breed stood out as dominant, so no one could say for certain what kind of dog it was. When someone asked him about his dog's breed, he would lift his hat and scratch his head, and say, "I don't rightly know. He just came wandering in the yard one day and he never left. The dog seems all right to me." The dog was always close to Johnnie, and when he was with a group of people, the dog watched from a distance. We never heard Johnnie talk to the dog or call him by any name, yet the dog was always with him. When Johnnie got out of his pickup truck, the dog jumped out of the pickup bed. When Johnnie got in, before he could slam the door shut, the dog was in the back, and Johnnie never said a word to him. So, on lonely acres lived Johnnie Walker, an ugly dog, and four mean mules, yet Johnnie talked a great deal about his sweet, loving niece and about how good she was to him and how she loved him. She was the only child born to his one sister, who lived in the city, nestled in the foothills on the eastern slope of the Rocky Mountains.

We often drove by old Johnnie's crossroads, sometimes on the way to church, sometimes to town or to the eighty acres of ground my father owned a few miles from our farmstead, on the other side of Johnnie Walker's place. We drove by often, and so did the rest of the country, and no one ever saw a vehicle that wasn't from our area in his yard. No family member visited him for at least twenty years. These kinds of things were talked about around our hills, and it would have been passed around if his sweet niece had visited.

There were ladies who sat on the phone's party line, with their earpiece tight to their ears and their hands tightly over the mouthpiece. Heck, these things were in the social columns of the local newspaper. Happenings, like who had company at the homes and who visited who, were an entire column and made for some interesting reading, if one cared about that stuff. It seemed to me that my mother only read it to find out if there was anything about us in the paper, and when the newspaper did print anything that had to do with us, Mom sure was disgusted. There was even a time or two when she called up the writer of that article, just to set her straight—I bet that was good listening for the ladies with their phone receivers attached to the sides of their heads.

Consequently, we knew that old Johnnie never went anywhere farther than our little town. He didn't have a telephone. If there had been any communication between the sweet niece and Johnnie, it would have been done by mail. According to the mailman, the letters were few to his mailbox. Many more letters went to a woman's name that we knew nothing about. Our mailman thought that Johnnie received maybe one or two letters a year.

Still, the lonely old man lived for the love of his sweet niece, and he horded his treasure for the one who loved him so. He assured everyone that his sister's loving daughter deserved more than he could ever give because of her love and devotion to him. And it happened to be that on his farm, he had a long, low shed filled with treasures—treasures he had collected, polished, and cared for with rough farm hands that seemed to soften when he touched the treasures. He worried over them and always thought someone might try to steal his hoard. The treasures? They were antique cars, each stunning by itself, but a row of these beauties filled the long building. They had shiny paint without clear-coat and gleaming chrome from the days when chrome was made of chrome and was not shiny painted plastic. I remember looking at three of them, but there were more down through the building. I was very young and only remember that there were more but not how many.

I stood on the cars' running boards to see in through the side windows. My brothers and I looked at a roadster of some kind. There was also a car that reminded me of the chauffeur-driven kind of car, where the chauffeur actually sits outside of the riding compartment in the sun or rain. Another car was small, low, and streamlined. I was too young to understand that cars came in different makes and models, but what stood out to me then—and still does—was their brilliance. I had never seen a car that looked anything like them. They shone like heaven. Dad must have put Johnnie in a good humor for him to show us these old cars—it was a one-time thing that he took the time to undo all the secret locks and booby traps that were designed to snare any bandit.

I don't remember Johnnie and Dad's conversation, but I was listening when Dad said, "You boys go around the other side of the building," where we couldn't see, while Johnnie undid all the catches and latches, lest we youngsters might tell someone how it all worked. The man was cautious. Once inside the shed, he had to unhook the battery-powered fence-chargers that were connected to the cars, meant to give any intruder an electrical shock.

The cars were beautiful. I remember liking the dark-blue roadster the best, and Mr. Johnnie Walker confirmed that the polished car might be his favorite too. Old Johnnie had a pleasant countenance and wasn't grouchy during the time while we admired his cars. It was strange not to see the mean look on his face to which I had grown accustomed. He was actually smiling, and that was the only time I ever saw him smile.

On a bright sunny afternoon in the mid-1970s, Johnnie Walker fell dead in his yard, a victim of an aging heart. No one was driving by, and no one saw him fall. Sometime later, one of his neighbors drove past and saw him lying still. The old dog knew something was wrong with old Johnnie, and in his protective spirit, he wouldn't let the neighborly man near the fallen man. The concerned farmer got on his CB radio and found someone to call on the telephone for help.

The sheriff was the first to arrive, but the old dog, which had always been gentle, turned fierce and wouldn't let anyone near Johnnie. The sheriff had no choice and had to shoot the old dog dead, just to see if he could help Johnnie, but it was no use. There was no pulse or breath. The mules were up as close as they could get—next to the fence; the quiet mules hung their heads and watched. The ambulance came and took Johnnie to the hospital, but he didn't return to his crossroads or to guard the treasure.

His kind niece, however, his only living relative, was quick to respond. Before Johnnie Walker could be laid to rest under his simple stone marker, with his solitary name and life's dates, she had the cars headed for Denver's best markets and had the plans already in motion to clear the quarter-section of land of any remembrance of old Johnnie, with the sale of the mules, farm equipment, and land confirmed. All the buildings were torn down, foundations dug out, dirt leveled, and corrals pulled out, and even the well where Johnnie drew his water was sealed and covered with soil, and the tower was hauled away.

Today, when driving over the crossroads, past where Johnnie's old home stood, no one would ever know that anyone had lived in a two-story house, or how the old man loved his sweet niece. Johnnie Walker was gone.

8

My First Crush

My first crush was Bonita. Her lush dark hair filled the width of her slender shoulders. Her eyes were dark brown, and she gazed squarely into my guarded eyes. I never thought she would look my way and never dreamed that she would notice me. Actually, before this moment, I hadn't given her any thought—Bonita was just too pretty. Still, she smiled, and I quivered inside. We played a board game in the county agent's back room, made to be a game room. We were the leaders of the county's various 4-H Clubs. Bonita was the secretary of a rival club, and I was the vice president of my home 4-H Club.

Bonita's father worked for the city and owned ten acres, barely enough to call a farm but still, they had some farm animals and a large garden. She entered crafts and foods in the yearly county 4-H fair, and I always entered, as my father expected, a Hereford steer. My brothers, sisters, and I always did well with our fat steers at the yearly fair. Often, we took top-honors. I fit in with 4-H. I knew innately how to grow and care for animals and vegetables, and I had confidence in dealing with the other members. We were, after all, members of the same thing.

Later, at the county fair, while the city folks looked over the livestock and projects displayed in the crafts building, Bonita and I and a few other 4-H-ers sat on the white board fence that separated the livestock showground from the rest of the fairgrounds. We came up with a plan to have a water balloon fight between us and the rival town kids. The local town kids never seemed like much to us country kids, but they seemed to want trouble with us—so we obliged them by soaking them with water balloons whenever they looked for us at the fairgrounds. Bonita's eyes twinkled when she smiled at me, and she spoke directly to me, as if no one else was present, as we all discussed the upcoming water balloon war.

Bonita was as good at throwing water balloons as she was at being pretty. She seemed to always know just how to dress and fix her hair. Her presence excited me, transforming me into an invincible hero of some sort. I was so good at everything in her presence, with an impenetrable self-assuredness that amazed me when I lay in bed at night and thought about the day. I had never been so powerful. Thoughts of her played on my mind and would have never existed if she hadn't gazed into my eyes, with her straightforwardness sparkling into my soul.

We doused the city kids with large and small multicolored water balloons, sending the failures back down the brick streets as fast as they could run. We country kids verified to ourselves that we were superior to any city dude who didn't know how to milk a cow, drive a tractor, or throw water balloons. When Jake come riding on his small motorcycle, making unmentionable gestures at us, we were prepared for him.

Bonita and I stood on top of the cab of one of the cattle trucks and hefted a ten-cent balloon—elongated and heavy. When filled with air, it was normally a foot long, but water caused it to swell to about four feet long. When the two of us threw this drawn-out water balloon, it landed beautifully over Jake's fuel tank, and his bike immediately died. He was left coasting down the brick street. Jake came running at us as soon as he could stop and put his bike on its kickstand, but we were backed up by more of the 4-H members, and our reinforcements pelted him with smaller water balloons until he was soaked through and screaming something that wasn't nice. Jake was last seen pushing his motorcycle down the street in defeat. Bonita squealed and hugged me, and I felt a contentment that was complete.

We ate hamburgers and drank "screwdrivers" at the concession stand at the west side of the fairgrounds as the sun neared the treetops above the western horizon. The lady dressed in a white sundress peered through the screen and said, "We have RC Cola, Coke, 7-Up, and orange soda, but nothing called a screwdriver."

"You need to mix all the sodas together," I explained.

The concession stand's white painted wood counter, which was lifted closed and fastened shut during the night, was great for leaning against as we recounted our victory. I leaned on my elbow and looked into large brown eyes that were already focused mine.

The livestock show was that evening, and as I led my white-faced Hereford steer, with its first blue ribbon hanging from its halter, I thought that Bonita would be even more impressed that I had won this prize. I wondered why I had this new thing of thinking of her all the time. I was unsure for a moment until I remembered her smile. I was fourth in line of because the Overall Champion, Hereford Champion, and Reserve Champion were ahead of me, in order of the ranking in prizes taken. We were leading livestock around the parade grounds in front of the bleachers, for the benefit of those spectators who came to see a show. Bonita was in the crowd, yet somehow she stood out, and I smiled when she gave a little wave and pretty smile. I was proud to have the position of first blue ribbon, but when Bonita smiled and waved at me, everything inside of me danced. It was as if I had the Overall Champion ribbon of life.

It took some time, but finally, the show was over, and so were all the festivities. The crowds went home, and so did our parents. I had to stay the night because I had a steer at the fairgrounds, and Bonita told her parents that she was staying with a girlfriend, to keep her company since her friend had a pig at the fairgrounds. The fair board required anyone who had a live animal at the fairgrounds to spend the night there. My folks went home to sleep comfortably in their own beds, but I had a bed roll to lie out in the aisle by my steer as it slept. At that age, the night air was great, and I could have slept on a mound of rocks and not lost a minute's sleep, so I didn't mind staying the night. I loved to sleep outdoors.

I had nothing on my mind but a little conversation, but things turned out a little different. Somehow, Bonita and I found ourselves all alone, sitting on a bench under some trees on the far side of the rodeo grounds. When she turned to me and kissed me, I was in shock, but I quickly recovered and returned the kiss. I was in love at that very moment. That night, we saw stars—a whole sky full of stars—and the moon came up full and splendid. I had a girlfriend who was beautiful and wonderful. There was no one in the entire world as wonderful as Bonita; she was life. Later that evening, when I laid out my bedroll by my steer, I was in heaven—a heaven ten times higher than the one the pastor talked about endlessly. I was vibrant; I was Hercules.

The next morning, I didn't see Bonita. I brushed down my steer and made sure he had plenty of water and feed. Other friends came by, but I looked only for Bonita. All morning, she was not around. Then, after I finished a burger and screwdriver for lunch at the concession stand, she came walking past—holding hands with Mark.

9

A Trucker Dumped Her Out

She sat on her only possessions—a few bags that were a little worn and manufactured of a canvas material in shades of green or brown. The one bag that wasn't green or brown stood out—orange with a wide blue stripe, but not quite orange because of how soiled it was. She sat with a straight back, intently watching the oncoming road that led to the truck stop. Her facial features were either Native American or the darker complexion of the Mexican people, but she looked more Native American by her skin tone and the shape of her nose, as if she were a descendant of Geronimo.

Her ill-fitting men's blue jeans were cuffed up about seven inches on the outside, exposing the lighter inner color of the denim. She wore more than one shirt, with the collar of a man's shirt sticking out of the top of her long-sleeved sweatshirt. This gave her upper body a smooth, undefined appearance. All this clothing had to be unbearably hot in the heat, but she wasn't sweating. She was expressionless, as if she had no emotions or thought as she stared down the road, looking for the driver who would give her a ride down the expressway. She sat on the side of the secondary highway by a Lower Rio Grande Valley truck stop, with the sun cooking her exposed dark skin an even darker brown, and her almost-black skin with its hint of red seemed to have had all the sun it could stand.

At seven in the morning, the beginning of my workday, she sat with her bags grouped together in the grass between the concrete curb of the truckers' parking lot and the edge of the black asphalt of the FM road (farm to market road). The temperature began at over eighty degrees as the sun came up over the mesquite trees—an occasional palm tree stood up high among the mesquite, as if a weird sprout. Then, after a few hours of sitting in the warming sun, she moved her bags, one at a time, to the other side of the Farmers Market asphalt road that crossed under the expressway, where she could face the oncoming traffic. In this way, she could increase her chances for a ride; her chances at shelter.

She kept all her bags within her sight as she moved them, and never stopped looking back and forth between the new location of her bags and the old one. When she was finished moving the bags, she either stood by her things and watched the oncoming traffic or sat on her bags, straight backed, with her focus on the trucks that came toward her temporary camp.

Her life was a simple one. Truckers often wanted company and of course other desires fulfilled, and they usually weren't particular about appearance; they wanted someone who was female and willing. This unspoken agreement between her and the truckers was the only bond she had with anyone, yet this agreement gave her shelter out of the elements in a rolling hut, whether hot, wet, or frigid temperatures prevailed. The truckers were always able to feed her, and she never went without anything to eat, unless she sat on the side of the highway too long before someone wanted her for a while.

She always was agreeable with the trucker in order to keep her life rolling on—not in an achieving direction but rolling in the direction of the best comfort she could achieve. This worked well, unless a man was mean, and she wanted out to try her chances with another man, or until it was time for the trucker to go home to his regretted wife and she, the vagabond, wasn't welcome. Her home was rolling around the highways of the states that are supposed to be united. The only unity in the states she saw, other than people always trying to tell others how they should live, which she avoided, was commerce, and she had no part in that.

She was well aware that uncaring people called her a "lot lizard," but this was her life, and it was better than much of her previous life had been. Now, she had shelter, food, and clothing. She did hate the thought that she might be confused with those who knocked on the truckers' doors when they left their headlights on, indicating that they wanted a little physical company and were willing to pay for it—to her, those were the true lot lizards, and she didn't envy their lives. She thought her life was a better life; she didn't ask for money and only accepted money sometimes, depending on the attitude of the person who gave her a few dollars. What she really needed was shelter and something to eat. She had nowhere to go and had only the days of her life to get through or endure.

I again saw her move her things to the access road around the corner from the Farmers Market Road, a little at a time. She sat out there for hours, but nothing happened. The truckers that passed did just that—they passed her by. Her motionless, intense state was obvious to anyone, as she looked down the access road of the expressway, between the exit of the truck stop and the on-ramp that was headed somewhere—anywhere.

My workday was coming to a close, and the heat had lessened a little bit as the earth spun its western hills around to the east, causing the sun to appear to be moving down over the hills. I hadn't seen her do anything all day but move around from spot to spot to the most advantageous spot for her lifestyle. She would keep moving until she was in luck, which hadn't yet come.

It was my birthday, and my lady had told me that she wanted to take me out for the evening. I was looking forward to a nice evening out, looking into her beautiful brown eyes and listening to all the things that are important to her. Of course, the dark beer, most likely Shiner Bock, with its smooth full flavor, would help my tension and stress diminish, as though I needed something other than this tantalizing woman to help me relax and smile, while at the same time stirring my spirit. She had a way with me, which was as solid as my stony heart.

But now, I looked out at this vagabond one more time, and I wondered if she had eaten today. There was a little restaurant in the truck stop that sold chicken meals, and that was little enough, so I bought a meal and a large bottle of water and took it to her. As I handed her the sack of something to eat, she thanked me and said, "May I ask you a question? May I ask you a favor? Do you have a little time?"

"No, I don't have any time. I have got to go." Then I said, "God bless you, honey."

Her eyes went smaller. She frowned a little, and she cast her eyes down and said, "Yup, sure." She spoke with a softening of the consonants, as did the Native Americans of New Mexico, but we were in Texas.

The sadness in her eyes because I was in a hurry to enjoy my evening, wouldn't leave me. I locked up all my construction containers and my construction office, but my heart kept bouncing around inside of me in distress. I couldn't raise my head to look at the day's fading sky. I couldn't do anything other than what I had to do. It was like God had a hold on me, with a lead attached to a halter around me—haltered like the foolish donkey I had become. I started my truck, and music came over the Bose speakers when the engine was running quietly and smoothly. I drove over to her—she was close to my passenger window, and I could speak to her without getting out of my comfort zone, especially with the conditioned air flowing out the vents in my dash. I pressed the electric window button, and she walked a little closer. I asked her, "What favor were you going to ask me?" There are moments when you are truly embarrassed when you do something or when you fail to do something, and this was one of those moments.

"I was going to ask you if you would watch my bags while I went inside to use the restroom. I don't want anybody to steal my things."

I told her that I would, while feeling like the back end of a talking mule for not taking the time to listen. I thought during the ten minutes or so while she relieved herself of what had to have grown uncomfortable during the hours she sat in the hot sun. This was after I had given her more water to drink and food to eat, not thinking about what the same foods sometimes do to my insides. I meditated on how good I have it and how blessed by God I am, and I realized that God cared about this woman who needed such a simple thing, and He wouldn't let me be happy or comfortable until I listened.

10

The Welder in the Yard

"Oh! The welder in the yard is frozen hard and a sorry sight to see. If I had a brain, I'd complain and be inside like you," I sang as loud as I was able to sing and still sing on key.

I sang in the welding work yard outside the frame shop at a trailer-house plant in a small Midwestern town. The tune that I sang to was "The Snowman in the Yard." The foreman leaned against the frame of an open door, watching me from the warm building. "You have a bad attitude!" the foreman yelled at me. I had thought up the new lyrics for the Christmas song just for this performance, for a single-person audience. My plan had worked, and the lyrics seemed to be wonderful to me. I knew at some point that Mr. Muller would check on me, and it only seemed appropriate to sing this very song.

Before the foreman got involved, I had it arranged so that I was able to cut the I-beam for the frames during the warmest part of the winter day. Then I helped my co-welders weld the frames inside the building during the coldest parts of the day.

In the northern part of the American Midwest, winter's temperatures would reach the high point at about one o'clock in the afternoon, which was only about thirty degrees during this particular winter. When we began our shift at seven in the morning, it was normally around fifteen to twenty degrees, and the early morning frost made the I-beams slick to walk on or work on. I thought it was unsafe to walk or work on the slick steel, which often wasn't as bad later in the day; but not Mr. Muller.

Sometimes there was a layer of ice to deal with or a blanket of snow. The problem with snow is that it is so inconsiderate as to fall on the areas where a person needs to work or drive. If the snow would stay in the fields and lawns and fall when it was eighty degrees out, snow would be awesome.

The leather gloves required to run the oxygen and acetylene torch didn't flex well in the cold, causing the work to be more difficult than necessary. It only made sense to cut all the I-beams needed for the next day right after lunch, when the frost was gone, and there was at least a little warmth from the sun, if the sun was out. Every morning, the needed pieces of I-beam for the frames were already stacked up. All that remained to be done for the frame to be built was to use the hoist to lift the stacked iron to the carts and push it in. This operation helped to not be out in the coldest part of the day. From the time I started it, this routine had always worked great.

The foreman decided that I could help with odds and ends around the plant that were not tied to the building of trailer-house frames. I was a young welder, eighteen years old, and didn't know how to properly stand up for myself against a man in authority and of my father's age. I didn't know my way around the rest of the plant and felt awkward when performing these unusual tasks. Other employees, knowing that I was a welder, would ask me what I was doing in their work area. I usually shrugged my shoulders and said, "Mr. Muller sent me over here to do work that isn't mine."

It took me a long time to figure out why Mr. Muller was picking on me and making my life miserable. Just before he took notice of me, I had come around to the back of the building during my shift, when I should have been working in the frame shop, to hide out for a moment, and I saw him with a young lady.

Mr. Muller was married and had a family. He had a couple of daughters that were older than Lacy the young lady I saw Mr. Muller talking with. At the time, it never occurred to me that anything was going on between them. I just didn't want to be seen going out of my area and hiding for a moment; he might think I was a slacker.

The other two welders Mike, John, and I were very fast at building the needed frames for the production of these mobile homes. We were always waiting for the crew who built the floors to complete their work, so that we could move our frame over to them and begin our next frame. I wasn't a slacker, and neither was the crew that I was part of. Yet ever since I saw Mr. Muller and Lacy engaged in a conversation, my life at work had become miserable.

Later, I thought that it was odd that they were out there, but I didn't place it in context until the end of the game, so to speak.

Soon, rumors were running around the plant—and around town— that Mr. Muller and Lacy were having an affair. There were a lot of jokes, like, "When he calls her baby, he really means baby." Yet as always, the gossip was entertainment for the folks of this small town area. Lacy was married also—not for very long but still married at the time of these goings-on. I didn't know her husband, except by name and face. He held a local job in the oil patch and seemed to be a decent man. Mr. Muller's wife was like most Midwestern wives; she put on some pounds with age and wasn't much to look at, but she was diligent in taking care of her family.

Lacy lived in the same small town as the trailer-house plant where we worked, which is one of the reasons the rumors started. Seems Mr. Muller's truck was seen sitting in her driveway a few times after the shift was over and before Lacy's husband was home from work. Both their vehicles were seen parked at the little lake outside of town. That was enough to fire up the talk. But I was only concerned about bringing in a paycheck and doing a good job, in which I took a lot of pride. I wanted to be the best welder, both with speed and quality of welds. Yet now, I was walking around the plant, half lost, and tightening a loose gas pipe or adding some screws to something that I had no interest in. I was a welder and knew that welding frames in a trailer-house plant wasn't the end. I had visions of welding underwater in the Gulf of Mexico, where the oil field was cranking up. Or was that the oil ocean? I needed the experience of being a welder so that I would be taken seriously, and this job was welding experience. I had no interest in the affairs of local life.

I had extra time on my hands, so when I could sneak the time in without being seen by Mr. Muller or any of the known snitches in the plant, I would weld together the punch-outs from the frame, pieces of welding rod, or other scraps of metal to form odd works of art. My coworkers enjoyed this and would be lookouts for me. Yet every once in a while, there would be a slip-up, and Mr. Muller would come around the corner and harass me about my extra work activity while on the clock. Before my seeing him and Lacy talking outback, it was only him scoffing and showing disapproval of my slightly rebellious ways. But things changed to where Mr. Muller thought I had time to take care of his problems, but I couldn't do anything about his real problems.

We welders were a team, and Mike, John, and I always worked together on everything. The walls on the sides of the welding area were only eight feet high. We welders were paid one dollar an hour more than the production employees, and that was well known throughout the plant. That created enough jealousy to make us a target. Consequently, we took some scuff from the other crews, mostly in insults or being ignored, which solidified our small union. A crew next to us on the other side of a wall thought it was great to throw their candy wrappers over the wall and into our work area. We had to keep our area clean, and with all the sparks we had flying around due to the welding process, nothing flammable was allowed in the area. We tired quickly of picking up their trash, and we soon came up with what we thought was a great plan.

We went to the iron pile and retrieved a four-foot–long piece of ten-inch I-beam. John and I held it up in front of our faces, with our elbows down so we could cast it over the wall, while Mike jumped on top of a welding machine so he could look over the wall, making sure no one was where the I-beam would land. When Mike said, "All is clear," John and I tossed the I-beam over the wall. It made an awful racket when the metal crashed against the concrete floor. All heads turned, and we went back to work.

Soon, Mr. Muller was in our area, complaining about our discarding trash (the I-beam) in our unfriendly neighbor's area, even though we didn't run to him like a snot-nose brat, as our not-so-friendly neighbors had done with their wounded-self story. The foreman had no sense of humor about our making our point to those who built the trailer walls next door. Mike, John, and I agreed that we had done the right thing because we never picked their trash up again. I thought that the respect we earned was good.

But soon, I was going somewhere to fix something that someone else should have done right the first time. This caused me to work a lot harder in trying to keep up my end of the welding team. I wondered, "If we made a mistake, like leaving off a weld, would someone else be required to fix that for us?" Well, we all knew the answer to that question.

Every so often, the company would buy a keg of beer for those wanting to partake. The keg would be taken to the local lake. There were enough employees that it didn't last long, but we enjoyed the pleasure. We noticed, though, that Mr. Muller and Lacy would disappear soon after we all gathered. Her car and his truck were parked with everyone else's, but they were not around. There were a lot of scrub trees in this lake park, with a lot of places to go and not be seen.

My problem was Mary. I worked so hard on charming her, but she was never charmed, at least not by me. My exhibition of exceptional strength and work performance never seemed to make an impression on Mary. She was quiet and kept to herself. She always took breaks with the other women at the plant, and I never saw her around town. Even at the beer socials at the lake, she hung out with the ladies and had a can of Dr. Pepper in her hand. She was always nice and polite, but I couldn't get anything else—no conversation. I even spun my tires on my old pickup, throwing gravel, but she never seemed to notice.

We welders had fun coming up with solutions to any issue that we came across. We had the trouble in the frame shop with our jig hammer disappearing. We only used it to knock loose the hold-downs on the frame jig after the frames were finished. The welding process always made everything fit tight in the jig because of the expansion and warping of the metal due to the heat produced. Our jig hammer was a two-pound sledgehammer head, with a piece of three-quarter–inch pipe welded to it for a handle. The wood handle had long ago splintered under the heavy usage and was discarded for the more durable steel. We were welders, and it was only natural to weld a steel handle to the head.

Somewhere around the plant, while I was taking care of Mr. Muller's problems, I found a ten-foot piece of quarter-inch chain. Since we only used it in the center of the jig that stretched out to seventy feet for the long trailer frames, we welded one end of the chain to the jig and the other end of the chain to the hammer handle, so that it couldn't disappear. It never walked away while we were in the shop, but during breaks and noon hour, when we weren't looking, the hammer would trot away to someone else's work area. It was odd how that worked. However, this chain secured the hammer so that it wouldn't grow legs and run away and was always there when we needed it.

Well, it wasn't long after Mike and I welded the chain to the hammer that Jake, from some other department, came walking down the aisle between the wall and our welding jig. We had, in the past, found the hammer in his area. Being the angel that I am, I couldn't resist feigning anger, and I yelled at him, "Don't you ever take our hammer again," and I threw it hard at his face. Of course, the hammer stopped at the end of the chain, a couple of feet from his blood-drained face. Yet that didn't stop the new lecture I received from Mr. Muller. It seemed he had no sense of humor, but then, Mr. Muller hadn't seen poor Jake's face. If he had seen Jake's big-eyed face, then he might have thought it was as funny a prank as Mike, John, and I did. We knew that we had made a point, and our paychecks kept coming in.

Most often, we took our breaks with the men who built the trailer's floor, and we had a lot of fun with them. We talked about NASCAR and the performance modifications we made to our own vehicles. We all had the fastest car in the area, but we were never challenged on the street, so that we could all hold the title in our own minds. Jim was married and never thought about building or modifying his broken-down old truck; he had other things on his mind.

I had my bag of cookies sitting next to me on the table in the floor-building area. When Jim walked by, he said, "Cookies!" Then his fist smashed down on my bag of cookies, and he said, "Crumbs!" Seems he was an angel, just like me. The laughter among the men was merciless, but I survived to pull a joke another day, and besides, cookie crumbs are good.

Spring rolled in. The cold, ice, frost, and snow became a thing of the past, and everything seemed to be coming to new life. But that spring, some things died. Mrs. Muller figured out the wind of change, as did her daughter, and it was known in the community that Mr. Muller was living at a local low-rent motel. The motel was where the storage garages sit now, but the old faded motel sign still stands as a reminder to those who cared that a low-slung motel had been there until it nearly rotted into the dirt. I no longer had to run to fix other people's mistakes, and Mr. Muller was quiet and kept to himself. No longer did he look on top of the world; his self-confidence was missing.

We didn't see Lacy talk with him anymore, and the rumors changed from where they were seen hiding out, to his and Lacy's divorce courts. Lacy was then living with another man, someone closer to her age. Lacy was very pretty and always had a lot of attention from men. Naturally, there was a man there when she wanted one. Mr. Muller wasn't that one anymore and wasn't with anyone. When he wasn't in his motel room, he was at the bar, where the old men hung out—a place with no video games or pool tables, only a bar.

Then came a morning when a company meeting was called, and Jim was announced as our new foreman. Great! I hoped he would keep his sense of humor.

11

For a Smile
(Clarence)

"Clarence, stop rocking, and let me go to sleep."

The empty rocking chair promptly stopped rocking on its own, just as it had begun rocking on its own. Travis rolled over and went to sleep, and slept until his alarm went off at 5:00 a.m. Travis hurriedly dressed, ran down the stairs and outside, to fed the calves and chickens saying, "Good Morning, mom," on his way out the back door. Alice, Travis' mother, heard another set of footsteps come down the stairs, and the water came on in the bathroom at the bottom of the stairs. When her husband, Mark, didn't come out of the bathroom for his breakfast, she called to him, and he answered sleepily from their upstairs bedroom, "I'll be down in a minute. I'm just having trouble waking up."

"Clarence must be at it again," Alice mumbled.

At breakfast, Travis's mother said, "It looks like you slept well last night."

"I did, after Clarence quit rocking my rocking chair."

"Maybe you should move the chair out of your room," his mother said.

"Maybe we shouldn't have planted the roses in front of the house." Travis leaned back and looked out at the roses through the living room picture window. The roses were growing beautifully by the front walk and were in full bloom. "I don't understand why a ghost would like roses so much, but he must."

Just then, the school bus pulled up by the mailbox, and the driver tapped the horn button. Travis grabbed his book bag and was out of the door and on the bus in a few long strides.

***

Four years earlier, Mark, Alice, and their son Travis stood in front of the house with Cynthia, who was selling the house, on the day which they took possession. Cynthia commented offhandedly, "If you don't plant roses. Then my grandfather, Clarence, won't bother you."

"What do you mean," asked Alice.

"Oh, Granddad was such a kind, fun-loving man. Even in the last years, he had a sense of humor that would crack you up. But he just couldn't grow roses, and he loved roses." Then she smiled, got into her Jeep, and drove away.

***

Seventy-some years earlier, after the "until death do us part," Clarence kissed his new bride and promised her quietly, "I'll love you forever and do my best to make you happy." Only the pastor caught this hushed vow, and his observing such sincerity moved something inside him.

Outside the little country chapel, Clarence's bride stopped to admire the roses in the churchyard. He watched patiently while she bent over to smell the roses and marveled at the pleasure on her face when she stood up and said, "Aren't the roses lovely?" When his love was ready, they walked hand in hand to his freshly polished Model A Ford, and he let her in the passenger side and closed her door securely. Clarence got in behind the wheel of his car and turned to admire his new bride. She was still looking at the roses she had just examined. She felt his stare and turned to him. Seeing his wonder, she said, "I've always loved roses but never have had any. Father thought such things were foolishness."

"I'll give you an entire yard full of every color of roses," Clarence promised.

Clarence was successful in fulfilling his lifelong devotion to his beloved, throughout the problems, challenges, and years, with the exception of the roses. His first attempt was at the house on the ranch where he worked as a hand when they were married. Clarence brought several wild roses, both red and yellow, from a draw close to the river because the price was right for a hired hand with a new wife. He dug them up, getting many pricks in his hands by the time he had them wrapped up in an old burlap sack and tied to the rear of his saddle. Every time he leaned back as he rode, he received pricks in his lower back, so he sat them in a stream that fed the river until his day's work was done. Then he rode out of his way back to retrieve them, in order to plant them by their house.

The sun had disappeared over the hills when he reached home, but his wife smiled when she saw why he was so late, and she didn't complain when, instead of eating supper, Clarence went out right away to plant the roses by the path to their front door—right where they could see them from the living room's picture window and where they would walk past them whenever they left home or returned.

The next morning, Clarence watered the rose bushes before the sun came up to bring the light of day, before he began his workday on the ranch. That evening when he returned home, he rode by the roses to examine them before putting his tired horse in her stall.

He brushed the roan down as she drank heavily from the stock tank, and then he hurried to place her feed in the manger. Clarence smiled as he took the tin pail off the fence post, dipped water out of the stock tank, and headed towards the roses. He had created a little dike around the roses so that he could put enough water in to soak down to the roots, where the water would do the most good. The western prairie was a dry place, and plants required plenty of water. This routine of early morning and late evening watering went on day after day, without fail. Clarence never tired of coaxing these plants to grow.

Clarence never had any problem getting anything to grow. He kept vegetables of all kinds behind the house and even planted vegetables in various places along the river and creek banks, where they were self-watered, to be ready for when he and the other hands made a meal while working cattle many miles from any of the ranch headquarters while staying at the hands' houses. His fellow ranch hands often commented that he could grow anything, anywhere; they thought they ate like kings, with the pheasant or quail they shot for the evening meals and the veggies that Clarence supplied. Therefore, Clarence approached the roses for his bride with total confidence that he would be a success, and his bride would smile at him with the sparkling eyes she had held for him at their wedding altar.

The leaves were turning bright and turning upward on the roses, and while they would not bloom that year, Clearance was confident that the next spring would bring some beautiful roses fit for his bride. Whenever Clarence rode across the prairie and saw any wild roses, he daydreamed of his bride's pleasure in the roses he had planted for her. He thought of the glow on her face as she looked at him at their wedding.

Winters on the prairie could be green all year, but they also could be bitterly cold for months. That winter was the latter—there wasn't much snow or moisture to help with the watering of the land or to temper the cold. It was bitterly cold from before the Thanksgiving holiday until the beginning of March. And the roses that had looked so promising that fall when they went dormant were brittle that spring. They had rooted well the previous spring and summer but not deep enough for the brutality of the harsh winter. Clarence looked forlorn each time he watered the plants and looked for life in them. The leaves never came back, and he grieved for the approving smile he longed to see on his wife.

Yes, she smiled at him for many reasons, but he never forgot the way she first looked at him when the priest said they were Mr. and Mrs. and then the smile she had when she explained that she loved the roses so. Clarence wanted to see that same dream-like smile once again. It was getting close to July when Clarence decided that the roses just weren't coming back. He'd always been able to bring any plant back to life but not this time.

The boss sent invitations to all the ranch hands and their families to join his family at the main house for the Fourth of July celebrations. Sure enough, there were steers and broncos to ride in the corral for the foolish and tough. The wise stood on the fence to yell and wave their hats. With all that commotion going on around the steers or broncos, the animals were more inclined to buck harder than they would without the commotion. Afterwards, the brave cowboys were brushed off with the stable broom so they could be civil while they ate under the elm trees with the womenfolk. There were a lot of jokes and jeering during the meal, with everyone delighted by the treat and wanting to make the most of it.

And dinner was a delight. There was roast beef, a hog with an apple in its mouth, every vegetable that could be grown on the prairie, and pies of every prairie fruit. Gooseberry and rhubarb pies were especially tart, as the hands liked them. The cherry and apple pies and custards were to die for, with the hot cream poured over them. All the hands were elbows and mouths, as they ate hungrily yet politely as possible among the ladies, throughout the meal. Then, afterward, the ladies helped the boss' missus clean up the dishes. Clarence had already been challenged to a game of horseshoes and was sure he wasn't going to play as bad as his partner had said he would. He was helping the men set up the game with a lot of discussion about the past games, mostly about the losers and winners, when he noticed his wife admiring the boss' roses. She held dirty dishes in her hands and walked back and forth, looking at the roses, without saying a word and with her dreamlike smile.

Clarence didn't play a game until she walked away from the roses. He leaned against a large tree and just watched his wife. His wife never noticed his gaze or how the other hands ribbed him about still having those honeymoon eyes. Clarence thought about those roses during the afternoon games. He has noticed when he sat by his darling at supper, the roses were in her line of vision, and while the spread of food before him was the best he had eaten in years, he still noticed when his bride looked at the roses as she ate. She glanced at the roses between conversations. While she never was impolite to anyone with whom they were eating, she never stopped admiring the roses—and Clarence never stopped noticing her preoccupation.

After the fireworks' last sparkle let the sky turn back to its deep blue, it was time to call it a day. The boss, being a just man, would not forget to say, "Good Night" to anyone. Clarence knowing this fact took his time getting his bride placed comfortably in her seat and checking the buckboard wagon and horses. Then Clarence pretended to straighten something at the back of the wagon. When the boss walked over to say good night, he found Clarence at the rear of the wagon. Clarence asked the boss if he could dig up a few starts of the roses for his wife's enjoyment, but the boss said, "Oh, don't you go digging on them. My wife will have my hide. But let me talk with her."

A few days later, the boss rode out to see how the branding and counting of the calves was going, and he called Clarence over. "The missus has a few roses dug up and wrapped in burlap for you. Seems she's taking a liking to your wife; otherwise, I can't figure it out," the boss said, pushing his hair back and replacing his hat.

"I'll be by after work this evening, if you don't mind," Clarence said.

"You'll be tired after working in this heat and dust all day."

"If you don't mind," persisted Clarence.

"Okay." The boss studied him in amusement and then nodded and turned his gelding away.

Late in the evening, Clarence rode quietly to the house, intending to surprise his wife with the roses, but then his horse snorted the dust from his nose. The horse's snorting alerted his wife and she came to the door with an oil lantern in her hand; she looked worried. Then, when Clarence spoke to her from the dark, she saw that he was all right, and her face became youthful again. Clarence threw his leg over the horse's head and dropped down in front of her. The roses were tied together and laid across his saddle, which he proudly pulled off for her examination. Once again, it was a very late night by the time the horse was cared for, roses were carefully planted, and supper was eaten—all done by lantern light. And Clarence didn't forget to water the roses before he was off to brand more calves the next morning.

Once again, the leaves filled the rose stems and turned toward the sun, under Clarence's tender loving care. He thought about his wife's pleasure when the roses would bloom the next spring, as the boss' wife's roses did every year. He wouldn't let his wife touch them, because this was something he was doing for her. The rose bushes were full of lush leaves when the fall came, and he found some tarp to cover them when the temperature fell close to freezing. The tarp was held up by stakes he had driven around them, so they had the strength for Clarence to scoop snow over them for insulation from the bitter cold that winter. The winter wasn't as cold or as long as the winter before, but Clarence wasn't taking any chances of the roses freezing out.

When he was sure the freezing temperatures were over for the winter, Clarence uncovered the plants and was delighted when they started to green up and come to spring's life. But the spring rains never came, and winter jumped right into a sizzling summer. The prairie was full of mirages, and he wore his bandana around his nose most of the time because of the dust in the air. He watered the roses every morning and every evening, but they still didn't seem to get enough water.

Then the grasshoppers came and ate them down to stubs on the ground. The hoppers hit them hard in the middle of a scorching afternoon, while his wife was trying to get their only milk cow through the heat—the Jersey had gone down and couldn't get back up on her feet. Clarence's wife didn't want to lose their only milk cow to the heat. They didn't notice the roses until Clarence pulled his bandana off his dust-caked face by her lantern light. They just looked at the rose stems, and then she turned to go into the house, Clarence followed her. He was too tired to say anything, and they ate in silence.

Every year, except for the year of the dust and grasshoppers, the garden grew wonderfully—tomatoes were juicy, carrots and green beans were crisp, lettuce was refreshing, and eggplant was a full of flavor. Calves were born and fattened up. There always were too many fat hogs and pigs. The chickens gave enough eggs to sell—everything at Clarence's hands grew bountifully, but not the roses.

After the boss went home to his Maker, the ranch was sold in pieces, and Clarence purchased the eighty acres with their house that had been part of the ranch, so that they could stay put. His wife said that she was accustomed to their neighbors and didn't want to understand new ones; she didn't want to leave where they had always lived. For fifty-some years, Clarence and his wife lived together in that same house from the time they married to the time they both passed away. She breathed her last breath in the bed in their upstairs bedroom while Clarence held her aging hand as if he wanted to hold her with him and not let her leave.

When she was gone, Clarence bought roses, with what little money he had left, at the new florist shop in town. He held the roses during the entire funeral service, while looking upon her lying at the front of the chapel in the same spot where they had said their wedding vows. Then, on his knees, as he was when he proposed marriage to his bride, he laid them on her casket just before she was lowered into the vault. After the funeral, Clarence walked right past where the roses had been tried again and again, and then Clarence sat in his rocker looking out the front room picture window until he died hours later. He just didn't seem to have anything to do, but look out to where he always wanted to grow roses for a smile.

***

"Mom, would it be alright if I brought the rocking chair to the living room; I think I would sleep better," Travis asked.

"Sure, that is where we found it when we bought the house," Alice said, "I have this odd feeling that it belongs there in front of the picture window; why don't you put it in the same spot we found the rocking chair."

Alice walked over to the spot where the rocker was found when they moved in and looked out at the roses and said, "Mark's roses sure are beautiful."

Once Travis put the rocker back in its place, it rocked every night and Travis slept better in his bedroom. Mark said, "I can hear that rocking chair rock every night."

"Well, Clarence was here before us and the other weird things stopped so I guess we can put up with him rocking."

Mark responded, "Seems right to me."

12

Gloves

Crack ... crack ... crack. I swung the heavy ax, doing my best to chop a hole in the ice-covered pond, while sending icy shrapnel into the crisp air or skidding across the pond's frozen surface. My breath fogged out in big powerful puffs to rival a car's exhaust. My brother, Mark, and I wore an odd costume as we walked over the hill to our frozen farm pond. We each wore black floppy over-boots pulled up over laced-up work boots, two pair of pants, and hooded sweaters covered with heavy patched coats. The crowns of our costumes were thick woolen stocking caps. All this was necessary armor against the below-freezing air and unbroken wind.

Mark had been quicker at grabbing the long-handled shovel, leaving the heavy ax for me to heft on our snowy walk over the hill, and now that we were at the pond, I was determined to get the glory of singlehandedly chopping the water hole for our cattle. Mark felt impatient with me, his younger brother, because of the cold creeping through his layered clothing during his inactivity. He asked, "You want me to chop the hole?"

"No. I'll get it," I said in between the slow, steady crack ... crack ... crack. I worked hard swinging the ax. It wasn't easy to grip the slick wood handle with my cloth-gloved hands, yet the gloves were needed for working in the cold and doing the farm chores.

After much discussion and effort, I finished chopping the drinking hole for the cattle, which by this time were standing on the bank, waiting for a drink. Then Mark scooped out the chunks of floating ice with his long-handled shovel. It was simply amazing how quickly the water froze into a thin layer on the black steel shovel blade and then evaporated away while in the unheated garage. It was a mighty cold winter.

The pasture land was hidden under the snow as we trudged back over the hill to our house. We followed our earlier footprints in reverse. The snow was perfect for sledding down long hills on an overturned '50 Buick car hood, but first we desired to warm ourselves and lay our yellow work gloves on the floor to dry by the big woodstove that gave off the best heat that any heating stove ever put out. Still, before we could stand in warmth, we needed to chop a couple of Red Flyer wagonloads of firewood and haul them inside for heat in our wood-framed farmhouse. The wagon was not a toy but used to haul firewood and such. My brother and I worked hard at stacking the wood just right to get the biggest load possible, to decrease the number of loads.

It seemed like the work was never-ending to us farm boys. There were cattle and hogs to feed and water, and chickens needed warm drinking water as much as their feed. The yellow work gloves we boys wore in the icy cold represented all this work. Because of this representation of work, I hated my work gloves and only tolerated them because they were necessary in this bitter cold. I was obvious in my distaste of the yellow work gloves and attracted some ribbing over them. "All you need for Christmas is a pair of work gloves. You do have work to do," Dad teased, with just enough merriment in his tone to let me know that he was only joking. Besides, I wasn't worried because Dad would always show his love at Christmas by giving just what he believed each family member really wanted.

Also, every year Dad would make a pact with Mom to only buy a mutual gift for each other and not give each other personal gifts because it cost too much. Then Mom would be both surprised and aggravated when she would receive an additional gift from Dad. Yet this routine went on year after year. I found this ritual very amusing. Such family rituals were the reassurance I needed to suspend any worries I might have about what gifts Christmas would bring. I knew that Santa Claus was a fantasy, and gifts depended directly on Dad.

Christmas morning finally arrived. The bare necessity of chores were done, and breakfast was devoured, while I could think of nothing but what was under our Christmas tree. My entire family at last was settled impatiently in our living room around the evergreen tree. Our tree was cut from a hillside of our Midwestern farm. The tree stood in front of the large south window, where it could be easily viewed from outside if anyone wanted to brave the cold for this privilege. I did run outside the first evening the tree was fully decorated, just to see its wonder. I wasn't wearing my winter clothes and was pleased as I shivered from the bitter cold that pressed in through my flesh toward my bones.

On the highest peak of this uneven pasture-cut tree was a tin foil-covered cardboard star. My oldest brother, who was ten years older than me, had punched a hole in the middle of the star so that the last bulb of a string of lights could be stuck through and he created a star of Bethlehem glow and sparkle; we thought it rather beautiful. A multicolored construction-paper chain, put together from the various chains we children had made at school and attached end to end, lay in between the gracefully looped strings of silver and gold colored plastic beads. Red, green, gold, and silver bells hung in their places. I loved the sight of the tinsel that was a reflection of the icicles that hung from the eaves just outside. All this was magnified by the larger-style colored Christmas tree lights. Some of the bulbs were older than others, with creases spiraling through the glass that danced reflections off the tinsel and ornaments, giving the tree a fairy-tale quality.

I sat on our front-room sofa between my brothers, Mark and Jeff. All of us were about as patient as starving wolves looking at a lone rabbit. We did our best to urge our sister, Kathy, to get permission to start handing out our gifts. Kathy held the high position of handing out the Christmas bounty, since she was the baby of the family. This was fine because that meant that we already had most of our gifts unwrapped before she was able to start unwrapping hers.

Then, just as Kathy was beginning to give in to our silent pleas, we were all bewildered when Mom said, "I'll pass out the gifts." We three boys all looked at each other in a state of shock at this change in the family ceremony. She handed me the first gift, all wrapped in white paper, with joyful Christmas trees all over it. The fabulous package was about five inches wide, eight inches long, and an inch thick. With all the restraint of an exploding volcano, I snatched the package but froze solid as my heart sank to the soles of my feet—I recognized the feel of brand spanking new yellow work gloves.

I thought Christmas was over. I'd actually received yellow work gloves as a Christmas gift! Dad hadn't been joking! Mom urged me to open my package. Dad said something about my not wanting anything, but in my shocked state of mind, I didn't quite comprehend what he said. Then, with all the speed of a turtle under a hot July midday sun, I opened what I knew were yellow work gloves. Everyone watched, and Dad was smiling with a glint in his dark eyes. After I stared with my watery, unfocused eyes at my unwrapped yellow work gloves, for what seemed an eternity, Mom asked Kathy to get a certain gift for me, wrapped in the same style of wrapping paper yet larger. Then, in my confused state of mind, spirit, and soul, I removed the paper from my gift, almost peeling it like an orange. When my eyes focused, they saw a yellow Tonka dump truck, coveted by any and every boy at my age.

13

Polecat

"Sam, you know you'll have to do what the schoolmarm says. You can't just do what you want, like you always do," instructed Sam's older sister.

"What she gonna do if I do whatever I want to?" questioned five-year-old Sam. Sam was used to doing as he pleased. He did his work like a little man—if anyone had asked him, he would have told him or her that he was a man. Sam wasn't his real name but as long as he could remember, no one called him by any other name. He was born on a prairie ranch—when you were out on the western end, the Rocky Mountains showed high in the sky. He had wondered at them and when he asked the older men, they said that they were like huge rocks that stuck straight up in the air for no good reason. "The mountains are hard to travel on horseback, and even worse in a wagon or buggy. And a Model T had an awful hard time getting up them grades. Be darned if you didn't push the car more than ride in it going through them mountains." The old cowboy spat on the ground and walked away at the end of that statement.

This was Sam's first day of school in the fall of 1924. He was proud to be going to school, but he also thought that there was work that needed to be done. He didn't know which was most important. "You'll find out if you don't do what she says," answered big sis. After all, she was a veteran of the last couple of years of the school sessions, and this achievement gave her the wisdom needed to give advice on the schoolmarm's way of doing things. So while the black gelding that the two were riding paced himself through the western Kansas hills, she faithfully laid her wisdom on her younger brother.

It wasn't long before they rode out on top of the hills to see the one-room schoolhouse out on the flat ground. Some of the kids from the area were already hanging around outside, waiting for the school day to begin. Mostly, it was girls, and this was distasteful to Sam. By the time Sam had the black horse staked out, the schoolmarm was clanging the bell, signaling it was time for school to begin. He hurried in and found that everyone was already seated, leaving him a desk in front, close to the schoolmarm's desk. Sam wasn't too sure about sitting in front, but he had never been bashful, and there was no other choice, so he took his seat.

No doubt there were many young men in the community who thought the teacher was something special, but to Sam, she looked mighty stern. It wasn't long before the Lord's Prayer and the Pledge of Allegiance were recited, and this lady in charge was saying that introductions were in order. Sam, realizing he was up front and that she was looking directly at him, stood up straight and tall, with his shoulders back, and confidently stated his full name—not his true full name but "Sam" and his last name.

"I'm supposed to have someone with that last name, so you must be Frederick," said the teacher, correcting Sam on his first name.

"No, ma'am, I'm Sam," Sam insisted.

"We'll use your real name here at school and not a nickname," instructed the young teacher, trying to create some authority.

"No, ma'am, I'm Sam. I've always been Sam, and I'm always going to be Sam," countered Sam.

With this debate, the school session began. The two disagreed from the start. The schoolmarm called on Frederick, and Sam answered. Still, they both diligently stayed within their role of teaching and learning. Sam did his best to keep up with the work around home, set some traps out for catching critters for their skins (the sale of which helped to keep money coming in the home), and to be at school every day.

Everything was going fine until one cool morning when Sam found a skunk in one of his traps. Now, any man worth his salt had his work done on time. With his sense of duty, not thinking about the strong odor of his prize catch, Sam skinned the skunk and salted the hide in plenty of time to be at school. His sister didn't think too much about Sam's scent on the way to school. She was used to his getting into all kinds of situations. Sam, with his determination to do what was right, didn't see why a little skunk smell would keep him from learning.

The schoolmarm, however, didn't see things the way Sam did. When the burning sensation hit her eyes and nose, she exclaimed, "Frederick, what happened to you?"

"Weren't nothin', ma'am," answered Sam. "Just caught a little polecat in a trap this morning."

"Out this instant, Frederick!" ordered the schoolmarm.

"But ma'am, I want to learn some more, and I am Sam," pleaded Sam.

"You smell like a skunk! Out!" she screamed, louder this time.

"But ma'am ..." was all Sam was able to get out before she grabbed the broom and came at him with wild eyes. Her swinging broom barely missed him as he ran out the door.

Sam didn't stop running until he was positive that the schoolmarm had stopped chasing him. *I didn't want to go to school today anyway,* he thought. Sam walked home, leaving the horse for his sister. He knew there was plenty for him to do at home. There were always chores, and the work was never-ending.

The sky was clouded over, and by the time he reached home, it had begun to rain lightly. After checking the livestock in the corrals, making sure that they had plenty of water, he went to the house to let his mother know he was home. All she had to say about it was that he needed to bring in some firewood. When he stepped outside, the sky had opened up, and it was in a downpour. He decided to wait to see if the rain would let up in a few minutes. He leaned against the house and stared out into the rain, thinking about that old schoolmarm. He just couldn't understand what the matter was with her. A little stink wasn't going to stop him from learning. He guessed that some people couldn't be understood.

All of a sudden, he was jarred out of his thoughts when his mother yelled out, "Sam, where is that firewood?"

"What a day," Sam mumbled as he stepped out into the downpour.

School proved to be good. It wasn't long before young Sam could read and do a few sums. He even learned about places he didn't know existed and that the world was supposed to look like the globe the teacher had on her desk. Learning our country's history and that it was a melting pot of people from around the world brought about the subject of nationalities. The schoolmarm asked the class to find out from their parents what their nationalities were, so they could report on it as a matter of interest.

Sam's dad, with a twinkle in his eyes, reminded Sam of a poem he had taught him, when Sam asked his father what his nationality was. And it did seem to be what she wanted to know. So when it came time for Sam to give his report, he stood up as straight as a five-year-old could and said,

> "I'm Scotch-Irish,
> polecat,
> and fightin' blood
> from away back!"

14

Snapping Turtle

Fish was a good change for an evening meal. On the farm where my brothers and I grew up, we had a way of putting fresh fish on the table. It was even a source of pride to us boys to provide the centerpiece for an evening meal occasionally. There wasn't much that we could call our own, and take all the credit for it during our early grade school years, but everyone in our family loved fish. We also enjoyed the fact that everyone would talk about how good the fish was, and we knew that everyone at the table realized we were eating fish due to our efforts. We didn't have fish every day, only when there was enough to feed the large family that sat down at our oak dining table. The only leftovers at these meals were bones.

The fish we delivered were mostly bullheads with an occasional catfish thrown in for a little variety. Yet we thought that the brown bullheads were really great eating, and the occasional catfish that we caught was a luxury. However, we had never eaten turtle, even though Dad often spoke on how good it was and that he had eaten plenty turtle when he was young—for a diversion from the usual possum that, according to him, with a slight smile and sparkle in his eyes, was at every meal he could remember during his childhood days. We hardly ever saw a possum, but every slice of meat on the family table turned into a delicious blade of possum, especially when there was a younger, impressionable mind sitting within the reach of Dad's fork. Dad would spear a slice of roast beef and lay it on the gullible one's plate and say, "Here—have some possum." At least fish couldn't be confused with any four-legged creature.

The way the feast was gathered was as ingenious as three bare-chested, barefoot boys—such as Jeff, Mark, and I were—could ever get. Our older brothers talked about trout lines (as they called them, but these were also known as bank lines, I found out later in life), and our only exposure to trout was on TV, where we saw some fool standing in hip-high rubber boots and flopping a too-long fishing rod and line back and forth. We Kansas-born boys knew that was a farce, since the fisherman never had his hook in the water long enough for a fish to notice it, let alone actually bite on the bait. The closer the hook and bait got to the bottom of the pond, the better the luck of catching a bullhead or catfish.

Then it was explained that a trout line was much different because it stretched from one bank to another, with hooks waiting in the water for an unsuspecting trout to happen by. Now, this explanation made a lot more sense than teasing the trout with a flying and flopping hook. But there were no trout in our pond, so we wondered how this was going to work out, and we boys contemplated this.

Somehow, we came into the possession of two trout lines, most likely by way of our older brothers, who were so worldly compared to us younger boys, who were restricted to the farm and had a little money to buy such niceties. During this process, Dad made it clear to us that if this was to be done, we would have to run these lines every morning and evening after chores were done—chores did come first. There were to be no exceptions, however, to whether the trout lines were run if they were going to be in the farm pond. Dad had no problem with eating animals or fish, but cruelty was another thing, and leaving a fish on a hook for too long was cruel. In our understanding, as we had always been taught by example, we vowed to run those lines every morning and evening. Past that, in our zeal we only saw platters mounded with tasty fish. Now that would be a true reward for our hard-put efforts.

In the lean-to of our wood-framed farmhouse, which served as our laundry room and kitchen, the trout lines were laid out across the floor. This was one of the biggest planning sessions and discussions that ever could come about on our farm. We were in high gear. I am sure that our endless chatter was a source of amusement to Dad, who was reading a Louis L'Amour book, and Mom, who was working on some stitching while the black-and-white TV buzzed in front of them. The important issue to be decided upon was the most opportune position to place these bank lines in the small farm pond, which was just over the hill. That was an hour-long discussion at least because each one of us boys believed he knew where largest fish resided in our small pond. Each of us believed in different spots. Most likely, they were places where each of us like to sit or stand while holding a cane pole or had happened to catch one rare large catfish. (The few catfish were coveted because the bullheads were never very big.) Yet that was not admitted; finally, the best spots were settled upon by how long the lines were and where they could actually be in the water when stretched from bank to bank. All of us boys knew that having the baited hooks in the water was extremely important (no fish lived on the bank), so there was a lot of compromise.

We didn't know what kind of bait was normally used to bait hooks for trout, but we had a good idea that we were still going to just catch bullheads and that occasional catfish anyway. Consequently, earthworms were still the desired bait because they were easy to dig with a long-handled shovel under the mulberry trees. Besides, we had been catching plenty of bullheads with the wiggly earthworms on our cane poles. This section of the meeting was voted on and amended much quicker. Life rolls on.

From the first day, the fish quickly accumulated. We boys didn't mind cleaning them, since we had grown up with it. The farm cats were kept busy during the cleaning process; guess they liked the fish guts about as much as they liked the warm milk at milking time. Also, we boys were amazed by how easy this form of fishing turned out to be. All we had to do was pull the line in, remove the fish, re-bait the hooks, and return them to the water. Later that day or the next morning, we were able to pull in the bounty. It beat standing in the hot summer sun with a cane pole in hand. Fishing with our cane poles was fun, but with all the farm work that had to be done, we didn't always have time to fish.

The days ran into each other, as they do on the quiet farm, until the unavoidable happened—we caught a huge, dangerous snapping turtle.

We believed this critter could snap off a kid's entire finger, if he was unwary enough to let the turtle clamp its sharp teeth on his fingers. A snapping turtle sure was a fearsome varmint that sent shivers down a kid's back when it snapped at him. I know because a snapping turtle had made me jump back many times.

We sure had a tough time pulling in the line that late summer afternoon. Two of us tugged on one end and the other guided the extra binder twine tied to the other end, so the line could be retracted. We had a good idea, as soon as we started to pull the line in that something was up. We thought we might have had a really large fish (maybe a trout), but it turned out to be a big, vicious snapping turtle, which would have been enough reason to scatter, if it hadn't been kept under control by the fishing line. The turtle saw us right away and tried to keep an eye on us, but there were three of us—no match for a single turtle. The monster was a dilemma but not unconquerable, we didn't want to lose the hook off the line; we didn't have the money to buy hooks, which meant we had to save this hook at any cost (the turtle's cost).

Mark moved in behind it and, with all his might, put his hands on its shell, threw all his weight on the shell, and held down this mighty finger-eater. Jeff grabbed the trout line, dug his heels in the dirt, and pulled on the line to keep its head from retracting into its shell. That left me smacking it on the head with a rock. Now, that may sound mean, but the turtle was dangerous, and we couldn't put our fingers in its mouth to retrieve the fishing hook while the turtle was still snapping. We liked our fingers the length they were already, not any shorter. The turtle had to be dead.

Little did we know that, to take the life of that critter, its heart had to be cut out. The monster (as we boys thought of it at the time) put up a fight that we couldn't believe; it tried to go everywhere. Mark had to work to keep the turtle from moving around, Jeff had his little heels dug in the dirt as solidly as any small boy could, but the turtle wouldn't hold still so that I could get a good enough whack on its head. Consequently, it took some time to end this fight between boys and turtle.

Finally, we knew it was dead; it had stopped fighting. Its head lay still and its lower jaw was split a little. It was now time to rescue the fish hook so it could once again be put into the service of catching the more desirable fish.

Now here was a short discussion: whose responsibility was it to take the hook out of the once-fearsome critter's mouth? It was dead—we were really sure of this one—but it was still a scary thing to put a finger in a finger-eating monster's mouth. I said that Mark should do it because he was the oldest and therefore the bravest, but Mark decided that the other trout line needed the attention. Jeff was not going to do it for anything in the world, so that left me. I didn't want to, but the job had to be done. I pried its mouth open and forced my little fingers down his throat, while keeping a sharp eye on its eyes, just in case they fluttered. Luckily, they didn't, and boy, was I glad. "Really, there wasn't anything to it," I told Jeff when the job was done. My chest stuck out a little further when I realized what a brave job I had done.

Now, it was time to get down to the real business—getting the lines re-baited so that fish could be brought in the next morning, to be the centerpiece of our evening feast. The thought was on our minds, though, that Dad would want the turtle. He told us many times how good turtle was to eat when he was a child. And now that it was dead, we decided we might as well take it home to add to the feast … until we turned to see the "dead" turtle crawl up over the bank.

15

How Could Such a Thing Be?

Did you see it zip slowly by
as it fell up from the sky?
It was the biggest little thing I ever did see!
How could such a thing be?

16

What Really Happened?

"Good night, son," Dad said as he tucked me in for the night. I lay in the low light of my nightlight and thought of all that had happened recently. I didn't want to think, but I couldn't sleep, so I lay there and thought. My father, older sister and I had just moved to a small, friendly town where everything was within easy walking distance. Our house was okay, but it was small, with only two bedrooms. I got the bigger bedroom because I needed room to play with my toys. My sister used the other bedroom, and Dad slept on the couch.

Life was simple and at the same time seemed very busy. My dad had to go to work very early in the morning, before my sister and I got up for school. One of the benefits of living here was that school was only three blocks away at the end of our street. Some of school was fun, but I would rather have played kick-ball or gone fishing. In science class, we were studying dinosaurs and how they lived, which was about the only part of schoolwork that I really liked—I loved to think about the dinosaurs' time.

At home, my bedroom walls were covered with dinosaur posters and above my bed was a shelf full of toy dinosaurs. My father had built this shelf for me because he wanted all my toys put in their proper place before I went to bed. In its center of the shelf stood my Tyrannosaurus rex the king of all the dinosaurs and he was surrounded by almost every other kind of dinosaur that had ever lived. I'd received toy dinosaurs as gifts on many different occasions. Just this past Easter, my dad gave me a basket full of toy dinosaurs with their eggs. No Easter bunny for me—oh-no, the silly bunny is for little kids. Well, the dinosaur eggs were really speckled, colored Easter eggs, but with a little imagination (of which I had plenty) the eggs appeared to be from a dinosaur. The eggs were positioned in a huge pile under the plastic dinosaurs.

While playing with my toy dinosaurs, I had imagined many times that they were alive. I decided the Tyrannosaurus most likely would be the boss because he was the king of all the dinosaurs. With such big teeth, he would scare the other dinosaurs, and if he wanted to, he could eat them. The pterosaur could fly and be the lookout for all the other dinosaurs, or it could silently swoop down on those it thought would be good to eat. They would all have their own personalities, and miniature dinosaurs would make cool pets.

Some dinosaurs were only the size of chickens, and I thought they would be easier to tame, although I have seen some ferocious small animals, like wild raccoons and possums. But it was more fun to imagine that the small ones would come running when called and then let me pet them.

On this night, the house was quiet, and everyone was asleep except me. *I'll probably be awake for a long time*, I thought, *because I am not sleepy at all*. I looked up at my dinosaur collection, with their ferocious teeth and claws, and I thought it would be very fun if they were alive. Their eyes seemed to be searching for something, probably for something to eat because they looked awfully hungry in my imagination. Then the Tyrannosaurus blinked his eyes and then scratched his chin with one of his front claws. I lay paralyzed in my bed as I tried to decide if he really had moved, and then he rolled his head and looked straight down at me.

Quickly, I jumped out of bed. *How could this be? He isn't real; he is only a plastic toy*, I thought frantically. Well, he may have been only a toy, but there was no doubt that he was looking at me. My thoughts ran wild as I tried to understand what was happening. We watched each other for what seemed like a long time. I wanted to wake up my dad or my sister. I wanted them to see what I was seeing, but I didn't want to take my eyes off the T. rex. I was afraid that he wouldn't be the same if I left and came back. He looked at me as if he were curious about me. He seemed friendly, in spite of his sharp teeth, and I couldn't resist touching him. I sat up, then got up on my knees, and slowly reached out to touch the top of his head. *Grrrooow!* He snapped at my hand and just barely missed my fingers. *Well, this isn't going to work. Hey, I'll bet he's hungry,* I thought. I ran to the refrigerator and found a chicken leg left over from dinner. My science teacher said that Rex was a meat eater, so I figured he would like chicken. Rex was the name I gave him; my teacher said that was Latin for king.

As I stepped through the door on my way out of the kitchen, something flew right over my head. I turned around quickly and saw that the pterosaur had landed on top of the microwave on the kitchen counter. He folded his wings and looked around the kitchen. Curiously, I walked toward him. Alarmed by my approaching him, the miniature pterosaurs flew to a safer place on top of the refrigerator. It was obvious I wouldn't be able to catch the pterosaur, so I decided to take the chicken leg to Rex. Rex would probably want to be my friend once I fed him, and I would be able to catch him. I reasoned that since dogs are usually friendlier toward whoever feeds them, so would be my future buddy Rex.

I returned to Rex with the bribery meat, and I saw that my Brachiosaurus dinosaur, which stood next to Rex, was looking around. It was hard to believe another one had come to life, yet I loved what was happening. The Brachiosaurus was not a meat eater, so he wouldn't want the chicken. That was good because I didn't want them to fight over the meat as I had seen dogs fight over food.

I climbed back onto my bed, and Rex growled at me. *Gosh, he sure is grouchy,* I thought. I cautiously held the chicken leg out to him. Timidly, he sniffed the meat, and then he savagely grabbed it with his long-toothed jaws. As I jumped back, almost instantly the Triceratops that turned his head and looked at Rex's meal. The Triceratops is a meat eater also, so the fight was on. Viciously, Rex and the Triceratops struggled over the chicken meat. Alarmed by the fighting brutes, the Brachiosaurus desperately tried to stay out of their way, but the shelf was too small for such a struggle. I didn't blame him for being frightened, because they were tearing into each other. The sounds they made were horrible. While the fierce battle raged, I looked for a way to help the scared Brachiosaurus. He squealed with fright and moved too slowly to avoid the bumps and shoves delivered by the battling dinos.

Rex, in his struggle to possess the meat, delivered a staggering blow to the neck of the Brachiosaurus. He toppled over and flipped off the shelf. He squealed with fright but then sank safely down onto my favorite pillow. He didn't move for a little while; he appeared too frightened. When he did try to get on his feet, the pillow was too soft and gave way under his weight. I could barely hear his frightened moans and groans as he struggled for stability, while the carnivorous competitors battled on the shelf above. I reached out slowly to touch him, thinking he wouldn't bite because he was a vegetarian. Still, I was careful—I hadn't forgotten the lesson Rex gave me.

The terrified Brachiosaurus timidly sniffed my hand, just as a puppy would, and then he rubbed the top of his head on my fingertips. This one was much friendlier than Rex and the Triceratops. I gently picked him up and stroked him lightly on his neck and back. He made a soft sound resembling a cat's purr. I thought I would call him Baro. Baro was a cool name and much easier to say than Brachiosaurus.

I was petting and playing with my new friend, Baro, when I heard an ear-piercing squeal come from the kitchen. It was then I remembered the pterosaur. I jumped to my feet and ran to the kitchen to see what the fuss was all about. In the middle of the kitchen floor was a scrambling mouse, which had innocently come looking for a midnight meal of crumbs. The frightened rodent was desperately trying to dodge the swooping claws of the diving pterosaur. I guessed that the pterosaur was hungry also and saw the scavenging mouse as a meal. The small gray mouse didn't like the idea of being a feast for the flying predator and was running for safety behind the cook stove. The pterosaur saw that his prey escaped beyond his reach, and after making a searching swoop around the kitchen, he returned to his perch on top of the refrigerator. He eyed the Brachiosaurus I was carrying, but I wrapped my arms around my friend, and the flying threat quickly lost interest, as this one was under my protection.

With the pterosaur presently settled down, my thoughts turned to Baro. I decided that if the other dinosaurs were hungry, Baro must also be hungry. I decided to get him some leaves from the bush just outside our back door. The warm night air rushed in as I pulled open the door. The pterosaur, feeling the fresh air, flew right over my head and out into the hot summer night. Baro trembled in my arms as the violent predator passed over us and made his escape. "Now what am I going to do? I'll never catch him out there," I cried, half to Baro and half to myself.

Baro wasn't paying any attention to me because he was more interested in the green leaves of the bush next to us. Reasoning it was impossible to catch the pterosaur, I turned to pick some leaves and fed Baro, who ate hungrily. After picking a handful of the greenest and lushest leaves, I peered into the darkness of our backyard for the escaped pterosaur. I could not see the flying fugitive, so I returned to my bedroom. There, I found a defeated Triceratops lying on his side, without any signs of life. The chicken bone was discarded and laying between the once-competing dinosaurs. Rex, with his rival defeated and his hunger satisfied, was looking for a way off the high shelf.

I sat Baro down on my bed with his leaves to munch on. I stood up on my bed and rose up high above the disagreeable Tyrannosaurus that shrank back in fear of my size. He growled and snarled his warning and prepared to defend himself against my giant form. I reached out to him, and in his fear, he tried to rip off one of my fingers. His defensive tactic was not totally without merit because I received a small gash on my middle finger. Since Rex didn't want to be handled, I sank down next to Baro on my bed. He enjoyed being petted and also seemed to like my company. The time spent with Baro was very relaxing, and I began to get sleepy. I lay down next to him, just to rest, while I watched him contently eat his fill of leaves. I must have fallen asleep because instantly, it was a sunny morning.

I awoke because my big sister was saying, "Sean, you only have an hour to get ready for school. Hey, what are those leaves doing in your bed, and why are you sleeping with your dinosaur?" My head was still foggy on the inside when she teased, "What are you doing? Feeding him in your sleep?"

I wondered if it was all a dream, yet there were the leaves next to my plastic Brachiosaurus. Instantly, I thought of the other dinosaurs on my shelf. I jumped up, stood on my bed, and checked them. I could not believe what I saw. My pterosaur was missing, my Triceratops lay on his side with a piece of plastic missing from his neck, my Tyrannosaurus rex was frozen in a defensive position, and the most amazingly scraped and scarred chicken bone lay between the harmless toys.

"Sean," my sister called from her room, "are you getting ready for school?"

"Come here!" I yelled back, "Come and see something."

My sister came in, hastily brushing her tangled hair.

"Look at my dinosaurs. They were alive last night," I exclaimed as she approached me.

"Oh, Sean, you are so silly," she teased. "You were only dreaming."

"Look at Rex; the way he stands is different," I cried.

"What happened to your other dinosaur? Part of his neck missing," said sis, with the look she has when she thinks something is icky.

"I told you—they were alive last night!" I exclaimed.

"Yeah, right," she answered in disbelief. "Anyway, you only have forty minutes to get ready for school."

I went into action when I thought of the consequences of being late for school. I dressed hurriedly, and quickly ate the Froot Loops my sister had set out for me. I hurried toward the back door with my backpack over my shoulder, where my sister impatiently stood waiting for me. I ran outside, and she locked the door behind us. We were hurrying across our backyard, when I spied something in the dirt. Against my sister's instant protest at the delay, I stopped to see what it was.

I was surprised to find my toy pterosaur, lying on the ground as if it had just fallen there, with the remains of a huge black beetle in its mouth.

17

Kindness Isn't Always Usual

When I was in the first grade, it was the first year of school for me because when I started going to school, there was no kindergarten class in my small town of a few hundred people. Mrs. Mayday was my teacher; I remember her as being pretty, well dressed, and small. The fact I knew she was small seems funny now, since I was only five years old and couldn't have been very big myself, but maybe I saw her among other adults. Maybe she was newly out of college because she did seem a little nervous and at times unsure, but she never was cruel or hard; even though she wasn't usually kind either. She never touched us affectionately or in discipline. She just did not direct much emotion toward the class of thirteen small students. The only emotion that I remember her showing was the day we first-graders learned that we lived in a country called the United States, and we had a president named Kennedy. I learned this new information because the principal of our grade school came to tell us that the president had been shot and was dead. Mrs. Mayday cried a lot, and we got to go home from school early. My brothers and I had lots of fun playing in the woods by our house.

The day I remember with the most fondness from those times in the basement classroom was an autumn day of celebration and of redecorating our bulletin board. The bulletin board was extremely important, as the school principal had committed the evil deed of putting us short people in a room where all the windows were above our line of vision. I barely remember the windows along one long wall because if a room could be tall enough to have a sky, those windows would have been up in the clouds.

I remember wondering at the fact that our little teacher remained as cheerful as she ever was, even though my overly ambitious classmate, Bob, who could think up stunts faster than two of him could carry out, had been caught and brought to her for running into the girls restroom, for the purpose of hearing their shrieks and screams. I just didn't understand Bob's need for causing chaos and wreaking havoc.

I found school to be a sweet change from the hectic pace of farm life. School was a place of order and peace. With Bob's mischievousness becoming a memory, our teacher brought contentment if not peace to our class by announcing that we were going to pull down the old thumbtacked pictures covering the corkboard and give it the look of Indian summer.

We carefully placed all the pictures that came down, which all had something to do with summer, in a cake box for next year's use. Our small hands then worked to cut coffee-brown paper to fit the board. More helping hands held the paper in place while Mrs. Mayday carefully pushed in brown thumbtacks, sorted from her amazing cup of paper clips, rubber bands, thumbtacks, and other small items. The cup was a magnet to my eyes, with my love of gadgets and things.

I was unsure of my place with these kids, and I wasn't sure that I wanted to know them, let alone get so close to them as to push my way up to add my little fingers in the crowd. So, I watched. I watched my classmates' eagerness, and Mrs. Mayday's efforts for order and neatness. I loved the coffee-brown color that was going up and thought it very fitting to have brown thumbtacks. I was content with the even shade of brown, as it fit my general mood and quietness. The bulletin board and I were complete and friends in this solemn state.

After the task was completed, she said we needed beautiful fall leaves to glue on to the paper. *Well, okay, I guess if you think it needs it,* I thought but remained still. She said that we would go outside, as a group and find the leaves of all colors—and I liked that idea. I loved the outdoors. I loved the tree leaves. I enjoyed picking out the biggest and most perfect of leaves, just to examine their uniqueness. I liked stepping on the fallen crunchy leaves, making a cornflake-like crunch—like smashing freshly poured-out corn flakes in the bowl—and the Rice Krispies sound, like when milk was poured on the cereal. I liked this combination sound under my boots. Leaves were great when the wind had bunched them up against a dirt bank in the dry creek bed, where there was enough to flop down into, roll in, kick, and throw in the air, as if there was a tornado, or just to lay in the bed of leaves to dream of unknown faraway places above or in the clouds.

Consequently, I was excited but subdued about the leaf hunting expedition our teacher described. We walked across the street to the huge trees of Dr. Hershel's front lawn. He owned the largest house in town, which was two stories of red brick, large front porch, and wonderful trees. The trees were so beautiful that I felt hurt twenty years later, when on a rare trip back home, I found the trees were all cut down, and only a barren lawn remained around a lonely-appearing house. It was autumn then too.

I searched for the perfect leaf, as my part in this magnificent project, among the leaves strewn around or in small piles. The bulletin board danced in the back of my head as I imagined the possibilities of patterns of God's gifts in fall colors. In my mind's eye, I saw the classroom wall display covered in all red maples, then brown elms, and other shades of various greens, browns, reds, and yellows of trees for which I didn't know the names. I personally always loved the huge yellow cottonwood leaves. They were great in their green summer's glory, rustling in the dry wind. They gave us shade and a warm symphony of gentleness as my brothers and I walked under them in the heat. It was greatly unfortunate that the mighty cottonwood tree had to lose its crown at the end of every summer, but like the shards of a broken crown, they were beautifully yellow, almost golden in the form of scattered leaves. Life's end fearlessly wrought.

So I searched among the big yellow leaves for the perfect one, a leaf without blemish, for our autumn board. I found the perfect one and, pleased with my find, I shared it with Paul and Peter. They also had good specimens, which reflected their thoughts of beauty or duty to obtain a leaf for the bulletin board. I privately wondered, since yellow and blue make green, if cottonwood leaves lost their blue when they turned from green to yellow in the autumn.

Then my heart felt as if it imploded and collapsed when brutish Bob's evil hand reached past me to crush my prize leaf. Forty years later, my ears still ring with the thunder of his wicked laughter at the expense of killing God's gift, just to see my facial expression fall. I was horrified and Bob laughed at me. In my pain, I ran and pushed him. My effort to knock him down, as low as my heart felt, only made him stumble backwards. We locked arms and only struggled for a moment then Maggie told the teacher on us, and we were scolded.

Peggy held a large red maple leaf. I thought she was pretty and nice, but her complete attention was on my crushed leaf.

I was back on my search for another king's crown. Peter and Paul backed off in trepidation from me after the leaf-crushing conflict, and I retreated to a secure within sight of my class but far enough away for solitariness once again, yet it was my ordinary state. Blown up against a large elm tree's trunk was an assortment of autumn's richness. I searched in this treasure trove but did not find what I desired. I walked along the path feeling like I had lost my best and dearest friend, and then a leaf blew down the path toward me and stopped at my feet. I bent over and picked up this one that looked like the crushed leaf, but it was shinier and completely perfect. I had found a magnificent yet plain yellow leaf, and it was unblemished. This leaf was much larger than my hands—bigger than both my hands together.

This king's crown was under my heavy protection. I could see Bob eye-ball my wondrous find as he held his scrubby brown leaf, but he wasn't getting close. I felt like twisting his ear off; and I think he understood my serious intent, for he lost interest by the time we stepped out into the dusty main street to go back to our classroom.

The journey back to school was uneventful. The girls huddled together in joint fascination about something that I didn't understand, and the other boys held their own society. I trudged alone to the side, and I noticed Mrs. Mayday's concerned glance, but she didn't say anything. I was just getting through another day, yet today I found a reminder of God's perfect love. I was joyful, and my cautious heart danced.

In our classroom, we again gathered around the brown bulletin board, but this time Mrs. Mayday was armed with a bottle of Elmer's glue. I watched as everyone pushed forward to have his or her personal finds pasted up first. Little Mrs. Mayday seemed overwhelmed. At last, everyone else's leaves were glued, even Bob's ragged one. And then she turned around to see me holding my prize close to my chest. She didn't know this was a king's crown, yet she seemed to recognize the reverence with which I held the leaf. She slowly approached me, I offered her the broad leaf, held up its stem, and she delicately grasped the stem with fingers that had pink pointed fingernails. She must have felt the sovereignty of the golden cottonwood leaf by the respectful way she placed it at the very top in the center, a position of honor over the rest of the leaves and safe from evil hands.

My heart warmed and rested in its peace.

18

Safely Lit

Incandescent bulb
Two hundred fifty watts
Lit our farmyard
to see whos and whats
It hung on the side
of a tall wood pole
in triumphant pride
under a green bowl
The bulb lit the way
To the chicken coop
Vanished all monsters
who in darkness snoop
It welcomed company
and saw them leave
Many a good chore
Serving as we please
Yet with a flick of a switch
the light goes out
leaving our farmyard
dark without a doubt.

19

Monsters!

The darkness filled the window in stark contrast to the well-lit house. I stood in trepidation in the lean-to that served as our kitchen. My father had moved the cabinets from the front room to this extended room one day while I was in school. I marveled at the change when my school day was finished and I walked in the house. It seemed impossible that something that looked permanent was not so solid. I was hoping that the darkness wasn't solid either and looked out the tall narrow window, the bottom ledge of which was low enough that I could see out.

I knew that it was totally dark outside, but I was hoping, as children do, that it wouldn't be that scary. I walked over and put my face up to the glass, held my hands to the sides of my face, and strained my eyes to peer outside. It was very dark without a moon glow. I remembered that the chicken coop door might still open because I was sure that I hadn't closed it. I hoped that I would be able to stay out of Dad's sight until after bedtime. I thought if he didn't see me, he wouldn't remember that the chicken coop door had been left open. Somehow, he always knew if it had been left open but would think of it after the very darkest of the night had settled in outside our cheerful home. I always thought it odd how the friendly and safe day turned into a formidable darkness, where the hope was drained out of me, and then sounds made me think there were a million things, both worldly and unworldly, ready to attack. It was my chore to close the chicken coop door just as the sun went down. At this time of the day, the chickens would have returned to roost after a day of pecking and searching for bugs and worms for their meals.

It had been a beautiful day, without unusual incident on our Midwestern farm. My brothers and I had been up early and ran the bank lines across the pond. A spring-fed pond lay just over a hill from the two-story farmhouse, and life seemed good as we ran over the hill with bare feet and chests. The early morning air felt cool, and our feet left dark streaks in the dew-covered buffalo grass. We watched for the known cactuses, which if even slightly bumped with our bare feet would leave our skin covered with a combination of long yellow thorns and short red thorns. The latter were the worst, since they were very small and almost impossible to pull out without returning to the house for tweezers.

My brothers and I had brought home several catfish and a half dozen bullheads of just barely eatable size. The fish were added to a store of fish in the family's freezer until there was enough to feed the family of nine. This meant that we had fish for supper at least once a week.

There were other chores that were not as much fun, like milking cows and feeding the chickens and hogs. The most special skill required in performing these chores was watching out for our bare feet. We boys never saw the reason to burden ourselves with shoes. Chickens would try pecking our feet, and the hogs and cows would sometimes step on them, leaving our feet bruised or bleeding. We were young, and we healed fast, so the injuries were quickly forgotten, but it was most undesirable to be stepped on by a two-hundred–pound hog or a thousand-pound cow. The soles of our feet were almost tough enough to be immune to goat heads and sandspurs, but not the tops of our feet.

Between the morning and afternoon chores, my brothers and I played in almost every draw and tree grove on the farm, including the blue shale hill just over the neighbor's fence line. One side of the hill had a steep slide of blue shale, which had a slight oily feel without actually being oily, creating a great natural slippery slide. This slide made the school's slippery slide seem short and slow. Also, there was the added bonus of no overseeing teacher, but we did see our neighbor standing by his large barn door, watching us play for a while. We played hide-and-seek, cowboys and Indians, war, explorers, king of the mountain, and whatever our minds could come up with. The only interruption in our day of make-believe was Mom yelling for us to come home.

Obediently, yet grudgingly, the three of us boys returned home, with fatigue weighting our legs down for the first time all day. We trudged up the draw and up the hill to the house, just to hear Mom say from the kitchen doorway that she was just wondering where we were. When I protested the interruption of our fun, she explained, "Well, your little brother is just two years old." Now, the youngest of our trio was a burden instead of an ally. However, we two older boys of four and six said nothing; we just played within sight of the house.

All in all, it had been a fun and adventurous day, until darkness enveloped the once-delightful farmyard of the daylight hours. Now it was filled with shadows and untellable creatures of the dark; these creatures waited in the dark and would love to grab a little boy like me, who had to venture out to close the chicken coop door. It would have been simple if I had only remembered this small task before the powers of the darkness came out. I shivered when I thought about what was lurking in the dark around the coop of sleeping old hens.

The trouble was, Dad never forgot anything. Then, the inevitable happened. Doom came when bedtime arrived, and I quietly tried to make it to my upstairs bedroom. Dad said, without even taking his eyes off the TV, "Isn't the chicken coop door still open?"

I was convicted. There was no jury who could set me free. The still night air was warm from the hot summer day, and I had only worn jeans all day. Yet now, I saw the need for shoes and shirt. Anything to delay the undertaking of a journey into the land of unknown monsters; there was the thought that the monsters would tire of waiting for me. I was only one small, skinny little boy and wouldn't make much of a meal for a huge horrible monster anyway.

When I was fully dressed, and there were no more ways to delay, I slid out, easing the screen door closed behind me, and pushed into the land of shadows and scary whatevers. There was no point in letting the screen door slam behind me and alerting all the carnivorous creatures in the land who were hungry for a meal of a little boy. Everyone knows that monsters are savvy creatures, even if they do live in the shadows. These monsters knew that if the chicken coop door was left open, a little boy was coming out and would be a great snack, if they could only catch him.

My feet were made of lead as I short-stepped my way to the chicken coop. I looked in every direction at once, as fast as I could, while I tried to discern the natural animal noises from the sly, nondescript sounds of the monsters getting ready to pounce upon me. Then, a wet muzzle touched my hand and sent shivers zinging down the back of my tense neck that traveled all the way to my heels. I was startled so badly that it took me several long seconds to realize that Shep, the family dog, had come to keep me company—or so I thought. Then ol' Shep turned back to the house when he realized I wasn't in the petting humor and had nothing for him to eat. It sure was a sad day when ol' Shep would abandon a poor defenseless boy to the horrors of the shadow monsters. But I had a mission to accomplish, just like a war hero, even if it did seem like a lesser task than rushing a whole troop of Nazi soldiers.

Finally, after what felt like hours of trudging quietly, carefully, and as watchfully as possible to the distant chicken coop, I reached the open door that loomed black above me. I tried to watch inside the coop as I watched over my back at the same time, lest a monster would be waiting to ambush me from just inside the dark of the coop door or from a shadow behind me. Then, quickly, not caring if the monster inside the coop ate all the chickens, I slammed the door, threw the latch in place, and streaked for the safety of the well-lit house that monsters didn't dare to approach. As I ran, I could feel their claws reaching out for me from behind. *Oh! If I only could run a little faster,* I thought, as the trolls breathed down my neck. I couldn't even breathe with my life in such danger.

I jumped clear over the concrete porch edge and slammed against the house door, while trying to reverse my momentum as quickly as possible, in order to open the door to gain the safety of my family. Then at last, I slammed the inside door shut and stood as calmly as I possibly could, with my heart pounding, since I had just escaped being eaten by the most terrifying monster that was never seen. My entire family looked at me, except for Dad. I tried not to breathe hard or fast in front of my siblings. Yet my older sister taunted me, "You're not afraid of the dark, are you?"

I was feeling very small, like one of those organisms we looked at under a microscope at school, as I looked around the room. Everything was bigger than I was, and everyone was grinning, even Dad, who was still looking at the TV. I saved face as well as I was able and said, "No, I just like to run."

20

The Tooth

One would have thought that the old codger had long lost any solid thought or memories years ago, by the way he spent most of his day in his rocking chair on his front porch. He rocked in a short motion with a tip of one sharp-pointed cowboy boot pushing him back forth while gazing off into apparent nothingness. Yet without looking in the direction of anyone approaching he always spoke, "Hello there," as if you were expected. He spoke with his amazingly friendly, crackling voice, which was accented in a strange but pleasant way that no one had ever heard.

The old man sat on his rundown porch in an old straight-backed rocker. All the finish of his rocking chair had weathered away and exposed the bare wood, which had long ago gone gray. The old man looked perfectly in place and at peace, sitting in his rocker with his long gray hair and beard. He wore round-rimmed spectacles without a nose rest, so they were pulled up close to his clear, alert sky-blue eyes. He was always a tad slow in turning his head to whomever he was speaking. Yet he had a way of seeming to look way down into someone's very central self, without appearing to be judgmental. It was more along the lines of understanding and thoughtfulness. He was never jubilant or jumpy, just content.

He lived on one of the streets on the very edge of town on a sand road with no curb or gutter. Wide but shallow grader ditches gave way to a large cornfield that stretched away on the other side, until the field gradually lowered to a creek that was lined with tall trees of all sorts.

At first, he gave me the creeps because he sat in the same place and in the same position whenever I walked to school, came home, or went on an errand past his house. There he would sit, rocking in perfect rhythm but not moving otherwise. Yet he didn't even seem to notice me as I passed, so I only kept an eye to make sure that he was always on his porch. Then, I started hearing what had to have been falsehoods about him, usually at the little café on Main Street where we went for Sunday morning breakfast. The old men drinking black coffee said this old man had been in existence since before the beginning of our town. The old men said that they heard it from their fathers and grandfathers, and the stories were said to have been handed down from generation to generation. The stories they told around the large table, which was reserved for the loyal and lonely customers, were outlandishly different from most of the local gossip—tales such as that he didn't know how many years he had lived or where he was born. When asked where he was from originally, he would point west and say, "Out there somewhere." Then he'd pause, as if in deep thought, and say, "But most of the landmarks are gone."

He was said to have joked about thinking that calendars didn't go back that far; at least, he didn't remember anyone having any or talking about anything that marked time from day to day. Occasionally, he told very questionable accounts about the younger days of his life, which were more than incredible.

In time, after hearing the stories about the old man and seeing that he didn't even appear to ever notice my passing by, I quit walking off to the other side of the road as I passed his weather-worn shack. His house reminded me of the slave shacks that were pictured in the school's history books.

Now that I walked up closer to him, I could see that he appeared to be a skeleton inside of his bib overalls and faded work shirt. He had the look as if he had once been a large man but now was wasted away in the idleness of old age. This most likely would have been the extent of my knowledge of him if a huge black dog hadn't jumped out of the cornfield and chased me right up on his porch. It had been an instant reflex; I was just looking for a safe place from the frightening teeth the mutt bared at me.

As soon as I was on the porch, the dog backed off and went back toward the cornfield, while repeatedly looking back to see what I was doing. I felt safer on the porch with the old man than I did off the porch, with that mean old scruffy dog across the road. The dog disappeared into the cornfield without ruffling the corn as an animal can do. I stared at the spot where he disappeared, wondering if the dog would come out at me again. The old man hadn't moved, but he broke the silence with, "I think she has a litter of pups in that cornfield and is irritated by people passing." I asked him if it was his dog, he replied, "No, I have a hard enough time taking care of myself. I don't need a dog to look after." Then after some more silence, he added, "Most likely a good dog when she doesn't have pups. Protectiveness can be a virtue or a fault."

I had never been around animals, so now I was curious. "What difference does it make if she had pups," I asked. "And if pups make a difference, does it affect all animals the same way to have babies?"

By this time he was looking me square in the eye, but not in a way that caused me to feel uncomfortable. He gave a soft chuckle and said, "Yes, even the dinosaurs of the long past protected their own little ones with more viciousness than they protected themselves."

I have always been interested in and loved dinosaurs and read all I could get my hands on about them, but I'd never known anyone who was sure what their habits were, since all we knew about them came from their bones and fossils. His odd statement told me why there were stories floating on the wind about him.

I asked him what he knew about dinosaurs and where he learned about them. "Well … well … do you really want to know, or are you just being polite? Maybe you will not believe me, as others don't, but I have no reason to lie." The old man both questioned and doubted me. His was a hard question, since I didn't know what my answer would bring. Yes, I always wanted to be polite, but I was also interested. Now I was really curious about what he would say, so I told him, "I have no reason to distrust what you have to tell me."

At this point he must have seen right through my answer because he started with, "Well, no matter. I'll tell you a little anyway. Pull up that old orange crate over there, and sit a little while, and I will tell you an old story.

"Long before there were any roads, houses, or even cities, this land had far more wild creatures in it than it has now. I remember an encounter with a behemoth with eggs to be hatched. Oh, wait a minute—I think you know them by the name of Brachiosaurus. Yes, I have seen those modern pictures of them in library books. They have got the shape about right, but they were hairy, like buffalo, and about the same color. But then, those who weren't there can't be expected to get everything right. Anyway, back to what I was telling you. My family and some friends were living in a cave because it was the safest place to be when the dinosaurs stampeded or fought—they would smash everything and anything and not even know they had done the damage. So there we were, kind of holed up, and it was time to go hunting for some fresh meat again, or we were going to get awful hungry, so my brother and I went out to see what we could find.

"My brother had a long, sharp wooden spear, and I had a knife made from the black glass we found from time to time. The glass could be chipped so that it was sharp. Then we'd wrap the handle tightly with some woven grass—not any grass but the grass found by the saltwater. If a man knew how to use such a weapon, it was as deadly as a modern-day steel blade.

"We came upon a nest of eggs that we knew belonged to the behemoth because of the light tan color and the small dark brown speckles. Since the mother wasn't in sight, my brother set about making a sling from small green tree branches and grass, to carry the eggs in. While he did this, I went to see what else I could find. Then, all of a sudden, there was such a noisy commotion back where my brother was working on gathering eggs. It alarmed me and sent shivers all through my body. I returned to find my brother backed up against a cliff, trying to defend himself against the mother behemoth. His short spear that had formerly looked so very long and sharp as it towered above his head now didn't seem like much protection. There he was, with no way of retreat, jabbing with his spear and dodging attempting to survive the lunges the huge animal made who was trying to crush him in her jaws.

"He was running back and forth as fast as possible, yet he still was cornered in the concave of the bluff. No way could he kill the creature from his position, since her head was hung low, and he couldn't reach her throat. Stabbing her head just made her angrier. Consequently, now was the time for me to act. All I had to do was dodge the behemoth's tail and scamper up her back by grabbing handfuls of hair and digging my toes into her hide and flesh. It was almost like climbing a tree.

"One of the hardest parts of my task was getting past her swinging tail, which wasn't swinging to hit me but swinging in her excitement. I could have been crushed or smashed by her lumbering tail—it was as big as a pine tree. Finally, I made a mad dash for her back, timing my run with the swinging of her tail, and then jumped as high as I could onto her back, grabbing handfuls of hair clinging to her. Normally, she would have started swinging her head around, trying to throw me off, but my brother did his best to direct her attention to him and away from what I was doing. The huge animal didn't even notice me; they weren't the smartest creatures, which is why they don't exist today.

"We ate most of them as the people's population grew. They were quite tasty when cooked just right—better than beef and healthier too. Scampering up her back wasn't difficult once I got out of the way of that flopping tail. The next part was the most difficult section of this struggle. I had to climb her neck because her jugular vein could only be cut up close to her head. Now, behemoths' necks were really long, so I had a tough job ahead of me but not impossible.

"However, climbing her neck was worse than climbing a tall tree in a terrible windstorm. I knew she would be very alarmed when I grabbed hold of her neck and would do her best to shake me off. It was, in a way, similar to the bull riders I have seen in the rodeos out west. Behemoths weren't very fast, but they could still give a man a hard time when trying to hang on to their necks. I had my legs wrapped tightly around the base of her neck, and I made sure that my knife was in place on my belt and secure. I shimmied as quickly as a man could go up a swinging, angry behemoth's neck.

"Behemoths didn't have ears that stick out from the head, as you know ears to be; they just had holes in the sides of their smooth heads. So when I got up high enough, I stuck a couple of fingers in one of her ears to hang on, which really irritated her but gave me a secure hold. I pulled my knife loose from my belt so I could cut her throat, and I tightened my legs around her neck. The behemoth's hide was just a might tough so it took several slices to get through and get it cut. Yet I did, and soon her blood was squirting everywhere. My brother—as happy as he was to see me deliver the fatal wound—was running around, trying to not get hit by the fountain of blood. Behemoths have a lot of blood, being as big as they are, and there was quite a mess before enough had gushed to cause the creature to slump to the ground. Meanwhile, I was doing my best to hang on to her, like a man on a bucking bronco. Then, at last, with a lumbering swaggering motion, her head fell downward as her knees buckled. There was the challenge—to tumble to a soft spot where I wouldn't hurt myself."

With a glint in his eyes and a soft chuckle, he told me about the extra soft landing, with his face in one of the huge eggs. And he told me how he rose up with egg yolk dripping off his face, and his blood-soaked brother laughing because they were such a mess. They must have been quite a sight. I wondered if it was possible for someone to live long ago during the dinosaur days and still be alive today. The teacher at school told us that it was something like two hundred million years ago when the dinosaurs roamed the earth, but I wondered.

I was sitting on the orange crate, quietly thinking about his story, when he asked me to go in and get him a drink of water, which I gladly did. I sped through the front door of his house. Only his screen door was closed, and it was on a spring to close immediately when released from your grip. I found the kitchen sink in the cabinets along the front wall of his one-room house and filled a glass that I found turned upside down in the drying rack near the sink.

I turned to run outside, but then I saw a necklace of large teeth on a stand next to his bed. I had seen similar fossils of the same kind of teeth in museums and recognized them to be Brachiosaurus teeth, but these weren't fossilized or petrified. This necklace was made of teeth that were old and dry but natural.

21

What a Day!

What a day,
when I pray
in my sphere so gray.
Colors bloom, expanding room—
from all God has to say.

22

When One Times Three Equals Twenty-Six

Financially, times hadn't been very good in the Colorado flatlands east of the Rockies. The expense of moving to Kansas hadn't helped our financial situation any. We had sold an eighty-acre farm and bought a 480-acre farm. In fact, money was very tight, and our family was dependent on food that we'd brought with us, whatever we could grow, and the few dollars that were left over.

Once our move was complete and we were in our new house, it was a lot of work to begin anew. The financial situation weighed very heavily on Mom's mind as she pondered how she was going to keep three meals on the table for the six of us. As she turned the meager potatoes in the sizzling skillet, she thought about the five loaves of bread and two fish that Jesus had broken for the five thousand. Quietly, she said a silent prayer, with complete faith that with God's help, there would be enough to eat, until spring brought the garden produce in hand. Even in the spring, when the vegetables were producing again, meat would be short. The cattle and other livestock brought from Colorado couldn't be butchered if a future herd and flocks were to grow. Then, on top of that, the buck rabbit and three does we hauled with us from the other state hadn't reproduced like we had hoped; not one little one could be seen.

The rabbits had been put in a big cement-block chicken house, and every time Mom fed the four rabbits, she always had the desire to see little rabbits running around. These rabbits, once grown, could produce more rabbits and, when fattened up, would be a nice centerpiece for a meal. In this missed expectation, Mom was always let down. She didn't have much time to spend with the rabbits, so each day she just placed the food and the water in the building and left. This routine went on for many weeks.

Yet in the face of this disappointment, Mom's faith that the Lord would take care of our needs was strong. Maybe she got this faith from her father. I don't know, but he always seemed to get by, and I don't remember Granddad without a smile on his face, no matter how little he had. How Mom came by this faith isn't as important as that she possessed enough faith to get through anything. Mom often said, "The five thousand that Jesus fed most likely didn't expect a meal, either. Not from so little." Also, occasionally Mom said, "I really don't know how the Lord will supply our needs or what is going to happen, yet I am as sure as I am breathing that something will come through."

***

The morning sun shone brightly from the crest of the green hills on the other side of the small valley where the farmyard was set. Mom stepped out of the south barn door with a pail of milk in her hand, as the one milk cow plodded on ahead of her and then rambled out of the corral toward the pasture. Mom admired her boys—the youngest, who was six, and his older brother, who had just turned eight, climbing around on the wooden fence that bordered the corral. The boys were talking about only things that the very young were interested in, and the sound of their voices made Mom chuckle. The quiet of the morning was pleasant, with its only intrusion being the boy's joyful chatter.

Mom wished for the rooster's crow, which would mean that they had fertile eggs from the hens, but still the sun shone on everything in a refreshing way. These times made her feel glad deep within and made belonging to such a place comforting, even in the lack. It was good just to belong somewhere. Dad was in the field, and when the breeze was just right, she could faintly hear the tractor. She listened to it as she headed back to the house thinking that the two little ones would most likely be awake by now. Then, as an afterthought, she walked up to the chicken-wire front of the old building, where the rabbits were housed, to see how the four rabbits were getting along. Rabbits are always so pretty, and these white ones were no exception.

In silence, Mom stepped up to the hutch so she wouldn't startle them and was thoroughly surprised to see many young long ears sticking up out of various holes that had been dug in the old chicken droppings, which had accumulated many years ago and never were cleaned out. Quickly, she carried the milk to the farmhouse, took care of the kids and the morning's dishes, and then anticipated Dad's coming in from the field for a mid-morning cup of coffee. Mom was excited about delivering the great news.

What a sight it was later that day—the boys were yelling and shaking sticks in holes with her, and Dad was catching the young rabbits in gunny sacks. The boys had a lot of fun chasing scared kits out of the holes, which were linked by a series of tunnels. When the chasing and scaring was done and the bounty was counted, there were twenty-two young rabbits, and with the original buck and three does, that made twenty-six rabbits.

God had provided again—exponentially.

23

The Cow Patty of the Snowball

An alien spaceship passed our solar system during our Paleolithic times. The aliens were running out of fuel, and they detected the fuel they required in our sun—you know, one of the gasses that make up the burning ball and are burning on a continual basis. They had a process where they could beam the needed gas from the cooler interior of the sun while on the move. And being on the move was what they had to do, since if they slowed down very much, they would ignite themselves from the intense heat and become a comet (which the cavemen of our world—as the evolutionists like to tell it—would have probably worshipped as it went by).

Being the space-traveling aliens they were, they had been out there long enough for Junior to be born and become a teenager. He didn't want to travel outer space like his parents loved to do, let alone be an alien. He wanted to be an artist and was continually painting murals anywhere in the spaceship where he could find a surface to do so. This made his father furious. He liked the spaceship to be its normal color, like from the factory. And since every time he wasn't keeping track of Junior, there was a new painting somewhere, he decided to teach Junior how to pilot the spaceship, just to keep him occupied.

Junior usually just appeased his father to keep his wrath down whenever he pretended to be interested in his father's instruction and lessons. Now, the father needed Junior to guide the spaceship while he zapped the fuel from the sun. When the crucial time came, the artist only half listened to his father; he was wondering how the wall of the main deck would look with trees and animals of some kind painted on it. So Junior totally missed the fact that he had to miss a couple of rocks on the other side of the star where they were getting the fuel, let alone that the third rock from the star—by his father's estimation—would be the hardest to miss. This would have been an easy task, if Junior had been watching what he was doing.

Junior didn't even notice the star go by; there were colors in his head. The fuel-loading was a success; the guidance of the craft was not. Junior just looked up when the third rock from the star filled his view, and they ricocheted off the side of our earth. This impact tilted the earth; its axis slanted at an angle away from the sun, not straight up and down like it used to be.

The earth shook with earthquakes, and the ice began to melt as the sun now shone on parts away from the equator and closer to the poles of the earth. Weather patterns were thrown off, and rain poured. One very old man built a boat big enough for his family and a bunch of animals, or life would have been totally lost on this big rock. These were the people who survived the flood, and that was good, but the man got drunk after the water went down enough that they could dock on a really tall mountain and get out. Well, one of his boys got cursed, and then there was a split in the family, as small as it was, and people have not been getting along ever since. But the third rock from the star still had people on it, and that was good.

The spaceship with the aliens was covered with a lot of snow and ice it had picked up from the third rock from the center star of that solar system. Even with the new load of fuel, the spaceship's propulsion system was too severely damaged to fight the gravity of the star. It froze up and became unrecognizable as a ship. It was caught in the farthest reaches of the star's gravity and started its lonely orbit around the sun, picking up all the moisture left in our solar system becoming a big ball of snow and ice.

Years later, a man in desolate southwestern Kansas with a homemade telescope—made mostly out of whatever junk he could find, like an old differential from an abandoned car and with some fairly good math skills—found the ball of ice. He called it a planet, and named the so-called planet Pluto, which is appropriate, since Pluto the cartoon dog was pretty silly.

24

Natural Occurrence

"Bang-bang!" I shouted at my now-Indian brother. He flung his arms up in the air as his body twisted, and he fell in the tall, soft cheat-grass. Then up came the shirtless boy, demanding to be the cowboy the next time, which could never happen, because I was the older brother and had to be the hero. I was the hero who daily saved the land from hostile would-be scalpers of the imaginary shrieking, trembling women and children—this hid in my imagination but definitely was real.

However, the discussion with my brother was interrupted by the pop-pop of the John Deere tractor Dad used to work the fields. My brother and I had dubbed the tractor "Johnny Pop," because of its steady popping sound as it chugged around our small farm. Dad, who was dusty and sun-darkened, wore a contented smile as he clutched Johnny Pop and shoved the throttle down. The tractor popped so slowly that it sounded like it would die, only to rev up slightly with each steady pop. Then, before Dad could pull the choke to finally still the popping, my brother and I had climbed up and were hanging with our bony arms wrapped around Dad's neck and shoulders. We swung with Dad as he hopped off the tractor, and while I released Dad, my brother still clung to him, giggling.

Of course, I, being much more mature and knowledgeable, got the rusty tin can from the tractor's toolbox and carefully, so as not to get burned on the hot exhaust, climbed up and dropped the empty green bean can over Johnny Pop's smoke stack. I understood, in my vast wisdom, that it might rain, and we didn't want water inside the engine. By this time, Mom was standing on the porch and laughing over the greeting Dad was receiving. Mom joked that it was hard to tell which one of us needed a bath the most. Unfortunately for my brother, the livestock watering tank was close because Dad put him in it and joked that one of us didn't need a bath now. This gave me the opportunity to step up next to Dad and grab hold of his hand. Dad looked down and said, "Hey there, young man."

"Hey," I naturally returned. *It's nice being the oldest boy*, I thought as I watched little brother splash extra water as he climbed out of the tank, feeling in charge and self-assured.

"What do you think about school tomorrow?" Dad inquired. I shrugged my shoulders in boredom because how difficult could kindergarten be with my great knowledge? Life had always been a cinch.

Soon, the day's sun hid over the western hills, supper was finished, and baths were taken. My first day of school the next day seemed a natural occurrence, and there wasn't much to think about on that subject. I just had to go to bed early and get some good rest, Mom had said. So, with a full stomach, I was soon climbing up to the top bunk that older brothers always slept in, since little brothers might fall out.

Morning came quickly. Breakfast was the normal cereal and banana. Mom had my bag ready with all the things she said I would need. Mom seemed so excited—she kept smiling and looking at me. Mom had explained many times that a big yellow bus would come and take me to school, and naturally, the bus roared up to the end of our short driveway where I was standing by this time. Mom nearly shoved me in the opened door to enter this bus.

Before the door opened, I saw sneering faces of older boys. My heart pounded. I didn't know there would be so many big kids. I didn't know anyone, so I found a seat all to myself and watched as home, Dad, Mom, and little brother disappeared from my window. Then, "pop," and my ear smarted, and before I could clasp my red ear, I heard, "Hey, Dumbo, can you fly with them flappers?"

─◈✖◈─ 25 ◈✖◈─

Country Barn Café

Surreal is the word I would use to describe this Christmas party. Our hostess was the owner of the Country Barn Café, and her party was at the same place. I came to this town of only a thousand people to visit my mother. If it wasn't for my mother living here, I would never enter the town or have reason. The town was just too small. The only commerce catered to the farmers, whose numbers were dwindling due to the farms getting larger as the farming tractors and equipment became larger and larger. The high-acreage farms meant less population in the countryside; therefore, if there was no reason for a county road, it was closed and farmed over. Many houses were abandoned and indeed, where there had been settlements and homes, there now were fields and pasture. Unless someone knew, no one would have guessed that families had been raised on these hilltops, hillsides, and valleys. The town was a place where one could hear a car horn honking clear across town.

The county sheriff, who also had the duty of watching the town said, "There is no need to be out on the highway after ten o'clock at night because most likely, I wouldn't see anyone for several hours, if I saw anyone at all, and they would be driving at least ten miles an hour under the speed limit." No one seemed to be in a hurry in this area, unless it was a teenager pushing the limits, as many pre-adults seem to do. There was only one club in town, which was really just another bar, but it made the local people feel better to call it a club.

Some years back the Sheriff's Department hired a new deputy from a large city. I guess he got bored with our small town because one Saturday night, he decided to pull the local boys over as they left the club to go home. He gave them a sobriety test, which they couldn't pass, and he gave out quite a bunch of DUIs, with men to be bailed out of jail. Well, the womenfolk wouldn't stand for this. "Those are our men and as long as they drive straight home from the club, then they are to be left alone," was their unanimous cry. Besides, those men would be in church with their wives on Sunday morning, so what was the harm? It wasn't like there was someone to run over or into, because with the exception of the men going home from the club, there was no one on the streets.

To get to this party, I only had to drive from the east side of town from out by the hospital, which was more long-term care unit and Band-Aid station than anything. I brought my mother with me to the party—or was it my mother who brought me? Mom convinced me to go to this party, and indeed, I would have sat in a recliner and snoozed to TV shows if we had not come to this small-town event. I helped my mother out of my truck, and she leaned heavily on my forearm with a tight grip. The look in my mother's eyes was a mixture of gratitude, for the way I helped her around, and frustration of needing someone to help her walk steady. This lady on my arm had milked many of cows by hand and had carried bales of hay and buckets of water to livestock with ample strength, but now, it was all she could do to carry herself short distances.

Mable saw us through the large plate-glass windows of her restaurant as I pulled Mom's truck up close to the front door. By the time Mom was gripping my arm, Mable was smiling at us, with the front door held out wide for our entry. Mable then busied herself in settling Mom and me and other arriving guest into comfortable seats, providing us with a coffee or iced tea, and pointing the way to the buffet of delicacies she had set out. The counter was loaded with desserts, homemade candy, fixings for Mexican-style hors d'oeuvres, and all kinds of finger food.

To reach the food, I had to reach over the coffee bar stools, which were normally used by the men in bib overalls and wearing caps advertising a brand of seed grain or tractor. The men sipped coffee and talked about rain, received or not, and tried to find their most clever remark to their waitress during regular business hours. Now, all the men were on their best behavior, with their wives and other womenfolk around them. The inconvenience of reaching out past the stools wasn't going to prevent me from getting a taste of the country fudge or Mexican hot sauce. I leaned against the stools and reached out, gripping my leather-soled cowboy boots tightly against the vinyl-tiled floor. I had been at my mother's house all day, sitting and talking about the old farming days, and this spread of wonderful flavors reminded me of all the food that my mother would place on our large oak dining table. Remembering the bounty of flavors caused me to want to eat all evening long.

Our farmhouse's dining table turned out to be an antique at the farm auction, but it was very practical for eating breakfast when we started our days before the sun was up and ended it, as the sun dipped over the horizon, with the supper meal—"supper," because Jesus didn't have the Last Dinner but the Last Supper—around the same table where we had begun the day. All nine of us could sit at this huge table comfortably, even as we grew into large farmhands. At all three daily meals, Mom filled the dining table with fresh savory dishes, and set out all the leftovers, which we loved, the ingredients of which had their origins in our own five-acre garden, potato patch, or orchard or came from our livestock pens and corrals. I never ate better than I did in those days. Religiously, Mom prepared pork for breakfast, chicken for dinner, and beef for supper. At dinner or supper, the main meat dish was complemented with platters of sliced tomatoes, cucumbers, fried eggplant, and apple pie or cobbler. We milked our own cows by hand and had plenty of fresh cream to heat up and pour over the hot apple deserts. Whipped cream cannot compare with such a feast as hot, freshly milked cream, poured over apple crisp or hot apple pie. At breakfast, the side meat—pork chops or pork steak—was complemented with platters of fried eggs, pancakes, and fried potato patties.

Life was good, and such an abundance of food only improved its quality. We never had much in material things, and everything we had was used and old, including our hand-me-down clothes, because, in those days, small farms just didn't yield the profit to allow a lot of store-bought things, but our meals made up for any shortcoming there may have been.

Mable's buffet was set in the same style. Everything you could ever want was there—and more. Life was different in this part of the country, and no one thought twice about a man opening a door for a lady or helping her with her coat. Matter of fact, these women expected a man to act within civil manners. Their reactions wouldn't indicate displeasure if a man didn't treat them with the expected civilities or respect, because that also would have been disrespectful, but in their minds, they would dub him a "dude," and this would have been discussed only among the womenfolk. The same lady would always be respectful, per their code, Toward the delinquent, but he had nothing other than superficial civilities coming. If the man was in the area very long, he would soon understand a better way of behaving and, without realizing it, would conform to the code. Life in this area was subtle.

These country folk weren't concerned if a person was good-looking or not or whether the person was rich or poor. If you conducted yourself per the code of manners and civilities, then you were invited everywhere. No meeting or get-together was advertised in the local newspaper or on local television or radio. If there was a social function in town, you just knew. How you knew was a hard one to understand because someone might say something like, "I'll see you Saturday at Mike's" or something close to that. But for this party, Mable had invited people as she served them, as long as an uninvited person wasn't present.

The café was packed with people of all ages and income groups. The banker sat in his red plaid flannel shirt and blue jeans, looking as if he had just parked his tractor. A farmer was dressed as a cowboy, with polished black pointed boots, big round belt buckle, and black cowboy hat. He looked as if he had just given the ranch hands the evening off and headed for town on a paint gelding. Some people were dressed as they always dressed but with their best clothes of the same style. These best clothes would become work clothes when the work clothes were too worn out to wear.

A young man, wearing a new denim shirt and jeans, with a bandana tied loosely around his neck, sat with his wife, who wore a blue sundress. During work hours, he would pull the bandana up over his nose to keep the dust from moving cattle or the farm equipment out of his lungs.

Somehow, his way of dressing never changed, and his wife would not have it any other way. He, like many other men in the area, wore a clean, newer version of his clothes when he was out on the town.

Soon, the karaoke machine was on, and the would-be rancher picked up the mike and sang Merle, Willie, and Waylon's "We Should Have Been Cowboys." A lady with a crippling disease sang Patsy Cline's "Walking after Midnight," while one of her friends held the mike for her. She sang with a richness that made me wonder if this wasn't what had really happened to Patsy. The banker sang a song and was as humble as anyone else, per the code, when we all clapped our hands to his personal rendition of a renowned hit. On and on, the local hits came over the speakers, and it didn't make any difference if the singer couldn't carry a tune in a bucket with a lid on it; we all clapped as if Merle Haggard himself had just sung for us.

Mable sang "I'll Always Love You," and we all knew who she was singing to with her faraway look. Five years ago, Jack had come to town from the Arkansas hills. He was good-looking, charming, and knew the code. Mable had been single for over ten years. She did well with her small farm and café. Much of the meat and produce prepared at the café came from her farm, which kept the locals coming. Her food was the best in the county, and the little café was always full at mealtimes, with the coffee drinkers filling the tables and talking between meals.

Jack recognized Mable's success and noticed her nice figure, even though she never dressed provocatively, and he charmed a lady who had resisted being charmed for years. She knew better, she later said, but it felt good to hope for more for a while. The thin scars around her neck were not as noticeable at the party, and she wasn't as jumpy. She was full of smiles and grace, much for the same reason as when we clapped and cheered in support for the worst singer in town. The town had clapped and cheered for Mable every day after they learned of her being taken to the emergency room. The party lines buzzed, and unrelated people waited in the emergency waiting room. When the hospital staff moved her to intensive care, her friends lightly touched her as she was pushed down the hall.

When she was physically stable enough to have a regular hospital room, Mable was allowed to rest because the town's people know the value of rest to recover from anything. Her room was filled with home-cut roses and garden flowers. Her visits seemed as if they were scheduled and indeed, in a fashion, they were. Without Mable being aware of it, her cook had kept the café open during her absence, and the folks, seeing the café lights turned on, came in to eat or drink coffee but mostly to learn more about Mable. Someone would say, "I think I'll check on her about six," or something close to that. Everyone knew that if that person said it, then that was what he would do. Therefore, there were never too many people in her room at a time and not too much of the time. Courtesy was a value in this community, so it turned out that almost everyone was in to see her at the hospital, but no one too much. Her visitors never asked what had happened or focused on her injuries. They talked about what was going on in town or what was coming up. No one let their compassion for her move from their hearts to their eyes either; they smiled and told her how lovely she looked and wondered if her steers were ready for the market or if the new library would be as nice as the town council said it would be.

Mable progressed under compliments and emotional caresses, until she was back in her apron, pouring coffee and taking orders as normal. If anyone teased her or if a man attempted to hug her in a friendly manner (as they had been used to doing with her), she looked blank and scurried away. Therefore, no one hugged her or teased her until she teased someone first or gave someone a shoulder hug.

Mable held her eyes on the floor and walked vacantly for over a year's time, and everyone cheered, with their hearts dripping with concern, and then clapped when she finished singing a song to a non-present man who had beaten her into intensive care. They knew she still loved him and didn't even wonder much as to why. They all knew that they themselves had loves in their lives that didn't make any sense. Love never made sense anyway, which is why they always said, "Love makes strange bed partners."

Jack came back to town after he had paid his debt to society. Jack was not allowed a room at the old hotel on the south end of Main Street. Instead, they bought him a one-way bus ticket to Kansas City. No one spoke crossly to Jack, and their eyes never showed anything but friendship (even if the friendship was superficial), but he also wasn't given the opportunity to stay. This was a peaceful town, and the townsfolk wouldn't condone anything but a peaceful solution. Out of sight was out of mind, so the idea of getting Jack out of sight was the answer. The way to do that was to refuse him a place to sit, in much in the same way as a fly is shooed out of the house rather than killing it. Jack wasn't allowed to sit or get a room or employment. The room and employment wasn't denied him exactly; Jack was told that the rooms were all full or were in need of repair (which wasn't a lie, since the occupants were always reporting a dripping faucet or such) and that there wasn't a job opening in town. Matter of fact, the employment situation was so bad, to hear his friends tell him, that none of them knew where they would get their next paycheck or meal.

Then the door was opened when a friend told him that his cousin could help him with a job and a place to stay in Kansas City. Jack was loaded on the eastbound bus with an address in his hand. As the bus left town, the housing and employment situation naturally improved, as if by divine intervention.

Life is good in a small town. Janice patted Mable on the shoulder after she sang, and Bill told her how good she sounded. Indeed, her grating voice had improved, and she looked around the room into the eyes of her friends. Mable smiled and teased Ben about the girl he talked about but no one had ever seen, and then she poured him a cup of coffee.

26

A Cousin's Ride

Supper was finished. Dad had already settled in his stuffed rocker. Mom and we kids were washing our supper dishes. Mom scrubbed dishes as she sang "Red River Valley" in a rich soprano, and the rest of us, ranging from too little to help to thinking they were too big to help, joined in the singing and cleaning up after supper, wherever we could fit in. This chore brought contentment and family unity, and the farmyard had already darkened, transforming the kitchen light into a friendly ally.

When it was time to clean up and choose our jobs in this chore, I always volunteered to clear the table, so I could eat all the leftover food. This was a wise move for a fast-growing boy, whose ribs could always be seen, even if my actions won me the prestigious title of "Garbage Disposal." We were past "Red River Valley" and in the middle of "If I had a Hammer" when the phone rang. Instantly, without command, we hushed our clamorous melody. In the silence, we heard Dad say, "Hello? Hi, Ruth, how ya doing?"

Mom quickly dried her hands and went to the phone because this was her sister. All of us kids knew at this point what the turn of events would be. Our cousins were coming for a Sunday visit. They lived close enough to come for the noon meal and spend the afternoon before they went home in the early evening.

Billy Ray was one of our cousins who would be coming to visit. Anyone in Kansas who is called by two names can't be "all there." The two-names thing was Southern; Kansas was caught in between the North and South, but the first and middle names together never caught on here. Billy Ray was a couple of years older than my big brother, who was a couple of years older than me. Billy Ray was always doing something to one of my brothers or me. He was bigger than any of us and didn't even have kindness for my little brother. He was strong and mean. He was a lesson, for us boys, ages eight to twelve, in sticking together and in self-defense. He could beat up any one of us boys, but he couldn't beat up all of us, and he couldn't outsmart any of us.

One time he punched me in the side of my head when we were only talking. Billy Ray just seemed to like to hit people smaller than he was. My brothers and I all promptly hit him and ran. Hitting him was not what we wanted to do, so it wasn't a hard punch, but it did get him to chase us. A couple of days before this incident, Dad had cut down a tree. On the other side of the tree was a hole, muddy and filled with water from last night's rain. The solid road was beyond that. We led him right across the trunk of the tree. We brothers jumped across the hole and were standing on the road, waiting for Billy Ray. We just knew he would jump over the tree trunk and land in the mud hole, and we weren't disappointed. We laughed until our sides hurt when he splashed, and we were still laughing as we ran, with him on our tails again. But Billy Ray couldn't run as fast, being water-soaked and muddy, making our staying out of his reach a mild trot. My brothers and I learned how to shift the victory into our own hands.

My brothers and I shared a 90cc Honda motorcycle that our older brother gave us. He was eight years older than me and was always gone for one reason or another; this time, he was fighting in the Vietnam War. When our hero brother came home from the fighting, we told him what we did with much animation, and he laughed. I think he needed the laugh. Our motorcycle was great, and we didn't have a problem sharing it.

Whenever Billy Ray came to visit, however, he wanted to ride it. He always wrecked it, and Dad would have to help us repair the motorcycle. Often, Dad had to weld a clutch or brake lever back together or help us boys straighten something out that had been bent. Of course, to hear Billy Ray tell it, it was always someone else's fault, or that rock shouldn't have been there.

The teamwork of we three farm boys brought on a set of events that still cause me to chuckle when I am reminded of those days. Our father, foreseeing Billy Ray's causing further damage to our Honda motorcycle, forbade us to allow our cousin to ride it. Now, we knew our cousin Billy Ray would demand to ride our motorcycle. After much discussion, we knew we had to have a diversion, and we came up with a plan—a plan that we hoped would dissuade him from wanting to ride our motorcycle but appease him enough to get us by. We knew he wouldn't respect Dad's word on not allowing him to ride it; Billy Ray just didn't have respect for anyone.

On the sunny Sunday of our cousin's arrival, we had our 90cc wonder standing on its kickstand and hitched up to our little red wagon (our version of a Radio Flyer) with a long piece of braided binder twine. The twine was gracefully looped over the bike's tail light and knotted to the end of the handle of the red wagon. When Billy Ray demanded to ride our motorcycle, we told him that Dad ordered us not to let him take it for a spin. Billy Ray said, "But he'll never know." Obviously, Billy Ray didn't care about our father's word, so we offered him the consolation prize. "Look, you can have a ride in the wagon behind the motorcycle," my older brother said, and then added, "It'll be fun!"

"I don't want to ride in no wagon," Billy Ray came back.

My older brother suggested that I take a ride in the wagon to show Billy Ray how much fun it was to ride in a wagon tied behind the motorcycle. I acted like I was having fun riding around in a stupid wagon and covered my frustration at having to deal with Billy Ray. It was boring, but somehow, we had to appease the brute. I had my hands up in the air, making noises as if it was the most fun I had ever had. Billy stood with his arms folded across his chest, just watching. When we thought he was softening a little, we stopped to give him a chance at a ride—nothing doing.

Little brother Jeff then took his turn. Jeff wasn't as good of an actor, but then, he didn't need to be, because for him, it was fun. Still, Billy Ray stood with his arms folded across his chest. I took a ride again and imagined that I was on a fun amusement park ride—imaginations can be of great benefit if used wisely. I don't know if I put on a better show this time or if Billy Ray was just tired of us. Anyway, he relented and seated himself in the wagon.

By this time, my brothers and I were not happy with having to work so hard at giving him a ride. Mark was on the throttle, and I was seated behind him, where I could keep an eye on our wary passenger. I have no idea why he was so distrustful of us three younger boys. Could it have been something to do with getting muddy too often, getting his hair cut with sheep shears, or getting some minor abrasions? I always have believed, however, that he was always paid very well for his bullying.

We had kept our fun in the barnyard until Billy Ray was seated. Then, in short discussion, we decided the county road was a wonderful place to go for a cruise. Our county roads were paved with white limestone rock and were never smooth, at their best. The best Radio Flyers never had much suspension, so by the time we hit thirty miles an hour, Billy Ray was screaming for us to stop. We didn't see any reason to stop—this was fun for Mark and me. The way we figured it, his yelling was normal behavior for someone riding in a child's wagon at this speed, at about a half mile from the house, we heard curse words from the wagon. We could not believe the names he had for us.

It had rained recently, and the road had what we called "washboards"—nice little grooves washed across the road. I looked back just as we went across them. Billy Ray's knuckles were white as he gripped the sides of the wagon, trying to raise his behind off the bottom of the wagon (and he was still cursing). We were approaching 40 miles an hour—was that upsetting him? He had big eyes too and was a little pale. Luckily for him, that was about as fast as the old little 90cc Honda would run with this heavy of a load of two passengers and Billy Ray in the wagon.

You might think that we had had enough fun with Billy Ray, but we were unrelenting. Three-quarters of a mile from home was a dead end in the road. My brother and I talked it over and knew that we would have to slow down to a crawl to turn around, and Billy Ray would have an opportunity to jump out of the wagon. Then he would demand to ride the motorcycle back home. We also knew, from experience, that he would try to pull us off the motorcycle and take it, and he was big enough to do it. We decided that if he couldn't get a hold on us, then he couldn't commandeer the motorcycle. He had a choice: he could either walk home, or take another ride in the harmless little red wagon. The obvious did happen. My brother and I stayed on the motorcycle, and Billy Ray tried to convince us to let him ride the motorcycle as he inched closer to us as he stood on the edge of the road. We were not caught unaware. When he was too close for comfort, my older brother released the clutch, and we jumped forward out of his reach.

We gave him his choices: walk or ride in the wagon. In his frustration, he said he would walk. We brothers knew better; he was not used to walking as we boys were. We weren't twenty-five feet before he was yelling for us to stop. Same scenario: Billy Ray wanted to ride the motorcycle, and we gave him the same choice, only this time, when we started to leave him, he got right back in the wagon. He told us to go slowly. Maybe we did tell him something that sounded like a promise but it wasn't, and it seems the motorcycle only had one speed: as fast as it could go.

We soon arrived safely home (with a highly agitated and pale passenger) and parked in front of the house. Billy Ray ran straight for the house to tell on us. It was hot summertime. We didn't use air conditioning in those days, so the windows were wide open. All three of us boys were standing behind the lilac bush in front of the house, wondering what the next turn of events would be. We were all quiet and listening. We all heard Billy Ray say something unintelligible and then our aunt's shrill voice said, "They did what?" Then the laughter roared out of the open windows from the other three adults, and we knew we were not in trouble. For some reason, Billy Ray stayed shy of us for the rest of the day, and we never had much trouble out of him after that.

27

Doritos and Snickers

Doritos and Snickers
Pepsi and cream sodas
But I remember a time—
Thrifty days so fine
And the real treat
Taste, oh so sweet
Apples, pears, apricots
Grown on our own lots
Juices running down my chin
Sweet reward as the first sin

28

Mom's Funeral

It was a plan; for Mom's ninety-first birthday, we were to eat at Romano's Pizza. Mom told my older sister, "All I want for my ninety-first birthday is to eat pizza at Romano's with all my seven children." Mom thought that Romano's pizza was the best pizza ever made. I thought the pizza was fairly ordinary, but this wasn't my party.

I was supervising the remodel of a Walmart in another town, four states away. I was also very fatigued. I was required to be on the job by 6:30 a.m., and most days I worked until 10:00 p.m. and sometimes later, and that was the weekdays. On weekends, I put in four to five hours each day. This job ran seven days a week, with all the actual construction happening at night. My night foreman was a pain in my tail. He continually complained, tried to undermine my authority, and expounded on how much better he was at being a commercial construction superintendent than I was. I simply responded that he needed to call the owner of the company and tell him; his issues were his and not mine. My goal was to get the job finished on time, under budget, and with quality. I didn't have time for his pattering.

I had asked my project manager for three days off for my mother's ninety-first birthday pizza party, stating that this event wouldn't ever happen again, and I wanted to be there to sing "Happy Birthday" to Mom with my family. The project manager obliged, by agreeing to be on the job site in my stead for the three days.

On Friday morning, I flew out of a small airport, where I had to walk downstairs, out of the terminal, and up a temporary set of stairs into a small aircraft. Then, the second, larger airplane dropped into a small Midwestern city, where my plan was to rent a car and drive three hours over to another small city, to go to a heavy metal concert with my daughter. Three bands out of Chicago were playing, I'd never heard of any of them, but I was attending with my sweet child, who would turn twenty-nine on the same day as my mother would turn ninety-one. *Quite an event*, I thought.

The plan: heavy metal concert on Friday evening, spend the night on the floor of my daughter's small apartment so I could see my three grandkids on Saturday morning, drive to Mom's, eat pizza with Mom and siblings at the noon meal, drink beer with my brothers and sisters on Saturday night, and then fly back to see the construction start on Sunday evening.

On the second airplane, some man talked excitedly about his being the first Hispanic to be inducted into a Hall of Fame for his feats in golf, back when he was a young man. I was glad for him, but he talked all the way on the last leg of my flight, and I just wanted to get some sleep. Once on the ground, I acquired my rental car and turned my cell phone on. A message popped up on my phone. The text was from my older sister, who simply stated: "Call Me!"

I maneuvered out of the airport, through the small city, and was on the highway headed for the western end of Kansas, I called my big sis, who is smaller than me and had been shorter for many years. I always saw my older sis as a hero, a friend, mentor, and motherly; when we were kids, she was the one who would pick me up and hold me when I was left in a pile of bruises, and she would cry when I couldn't cry, but that was long ago. I figured that she just wanted to make sure that I was okay or had made it into the state okay, as she often worried about her little brother.

After the greetings, my sister said, "You need to stop by and see Mom."

"Well, sis, I am already going to be about thirty minutes late for the concert with my kid." The concert was part of the plan.

Sis said—in a tone she often used on me when I balked at doing something on the farm when we were kids, motherly yet authoritative— "You need to stop to see your mom first."

"Okay, okay!" I responded. I thought it odd that she could still have that effect on me, but then I also knew something was up.

I still debated about stopping at Mom's. I was trying to pack a lot into these three tiring days off work. But when I came to Mom's town, I turned off the highway onto the street that would lead to Mom's assisted-living apartment. Her apartment was small—kitchen, dining room, living room, and bedroom, all in one room and smaller than many of the motel rooms I'd rented on my work travels around this country.

I pulled up in front of the assisted living home, and parked the little rental car. Then I entered the building through the double doors under the front canopy. A woman employee met me in the front area, which was like a living room area on the left and dining area, much like a church banquet hall, on the right. She said that Mom was no longer in her apartment but in a room. I was beyond tired and was running on spirit rather than energy, but still, I walked down the hall to Mother's room. Her head was elevated in a hospital bed. Her TV was turned off, and the mini-blinds were open. The setting sun was down behind the rest of the building, so the light coming in the large windows was easy on the eyes. Mom appeared to be asleep. Her thin hands lay one on top of the other across her abdomen.

I stepped up next to Mom, between her bed and large windows, and lay my right hand over Mom's hands. I noticed that I was able to hide both her hands underneath one of my own hands. When I said, "Hey, Mom," she turned her head toward me and opened her eyes. Mom's eyes were sapphire blue, rather than her hazel eyes. Mom now had the eyes that I called "death eyes," as the elderly usually get in their last few days. I leaned over and kissed Mom on her right cheek and said, "I love you, Mom."

"I love you," Mom whispered. I wouldn't have caught her last words to me if I hadn't been so close to her face. Mom seemed to relax and had a contented expression, with her slight smile.

I stood there while the woman who always loved me slept. I watched Mom for a long time. I was torn between watching Mom sleep and going to meet my daughter. After a time, I backed out of the room and walked out of the building in a state of shock—my mom was dying, and no matter how many times my brain told my heart that this was it, and Mom was leaving, my heart refused to believe.

***

Unnoticed treeless plains swept by the little rental car on the drive from Mom's town to my daughter's small city. I drove into town on the highway that cuts through the Old Soldier's Home and then turns into a street that comes into the small city. My body was somewhat numb from fatigue, I had a concert to attend with my kid, and Mom was dying. My mind was overloaded, and I was operating as if on autopilot.

The stoplight was red when I approached the crossing bypass. I stopped before the wide white line on the pavement, with my foot pressing down on the brake pedal of this unfamiliar car. Sometime later—I am not sure how much later—I woke up with my foot still on the brake and wondering how many light changes I had slept through. I uttered a short prayer of thanks for the Lord not letting my foot slip off the brake pedal. I've never understood why the Lord takes care of me, but it is evident that He likes me well enough to do so. My turn signal was still clicking, so I released the brake and accelerated under the green hanging light, turning left toward the newly built dirt-car racetrack on the south side of town, where the metal bands would do their best to entertain us. I was careful to keep my eyes open at the four-way stop, knowing that I only had a mile or so to drive. I think that the nap at the last stoplight helped, and I felt a little refreshed. My body desired a nice clean bed at this point, and it wouldn't matter what was surrounding that bed. I would have been like a dead man in my slumber, but I wasn't about to disappoint my daughter. I was grateful for every moment I was able to spend with those who are important to me, and this time with my child was going to happen, if at all possible.

Somewhere inside of me was a boiling grief, and I hadn't had any time to process the fact that my mom was dying. My emotions were raw and molten, like a sleeping volcano, daring my fractured skin containing my turmoil to give away and let it spray, but on the other hand, my mother's quiet power tempered me and my exterior cooled, sealing off my emotional upheaval.

I parked the car in the graveled lot just in time to hear the end of a loud song, then a woman said something into a microphone, and then all was silent. There was a ticket hut, the same one they used for the car races, I supposed. Sure enough, I was able to purchase a wristband in order to enter, as well as some tickets to purchase beer. My mind couldn't do the math of how many tickets to buy so I purchased the amount the smiling young lady sitting on the stool behind the glass suggested.

My daughter's birthday twenty-nine years ago was extraordinary, at least to me. I didn't want any children the entire time her mother was carrying her. I was too busy partying and doing whatever I pleased. I didn't want to be bothered with a child. Besides, I had no idea how to raise a child and didn't want to learn. As the due day approached, all I could think about was this coming child and how this would change life—my life; it had always been my life. Then, this little girl was born, and I held this little wonder, and suddenly, I loved her so much that I was afraid for the first time in my life—I mean, truly afraid. I was afraid that something might hurt this child; there were dangers that had been just events, like the tornados that usually bounced out in the pastures, bad people, and the kind of stuff reported on the five o'clock news, but I never paid any attention to it until now. When the *wow* wore off, I thought I should call my mother and tell her that I had a little girl.

These were the days before cell phones. I dialed the hospital's phone that sat on the bed stand next to my daughter's mother's bed, and my mother answered. I am sure I seemed excited as I told her about this wonder of a child, and she laughed and said, "Well, this is happy birthday to me. What a wonderful present!"

I had forgotten my mother's birthday with all these new child happenings. I always tried not to forget my mother's *anything*, but she seemed very happy for this gift. It wasn't her first grandchild and neither was she her last, but my little girl was the first and only one born on her birthday. What a day; what a birthday.

I turned and walked toward the gate, and my brunette-turned-blonde daughter had her arms out to greet me on the other side. To me, it was like entering heaven's gate, seeing someone I love so much welcoming me. I was home. Her friend Juan was with her and seemed content just to be there. My daughter thought it was better that she not go out alone, and Juan always looked out for her. I wondered about his feelings for my daughter and how strong those feelings might be. It was hard to tell if he only had a protective spirit or was in love with her. I watched him and decided that he was blessed with a protective spirit and most likely was listening to God, even when he didn't know he was listening. I thought well of him simply because I love whoever loves those I love and does well by them.

I think that is what the Lord meant when he said something to that effect in Revelations, when He separated the goats from the sheep: "Whoever does for the least of mine ..." I was full of joy to see my daughter radiant and beaming. The weight of my work stress load had not dissipated much or the unconquered understanding that Mom was in her last hours of her life been dealt with, yet my daughter's presence eased all that was wrong.

We all want our mothers to live forever, without aging. Imagining life without my mother was unimaginable, but I was to find out it was doable.

My daughter was so very happy to be celebrating her twenty-ninth birthday with her dad at a heavy metal concert. All young people want to believe that their parents are cool, and this was part of it. I understood more about what was going on than my daughter did. She would understand when she reached my age, and she would do similar things with her children. This was a good time— a wonderful time. I didn't tell my daughter that I would have preferred to sit in a lawn chair at the rear of the crowd, where distance from the band tempered the volume and intensity, and where I could enjoy the concert in a relaxed state. Neither did I tell her that our quiet times together were more precious to me— times like when she and I went on walks around the block, and I listened to her talk about what was going on in her life, good or bad. And I certainly didn't tell her that her grandma was breathing her last breaths while we partied. I gained fortitude in knowing that Mom always put everyone else ahead of herself, and I tried to do the same; I put my daughter's happiness ahead of my feelings by the living example my mother had always given me. I imagined that if Mom could speak, she would have told us to go and have some fun, and she'd have said it with her smile.

I simply told my daughter that her grandmother was not doing well. Her grandmother had had many "spells" (heart attacks and such) over the years—Mom called her health issues "spells," so spells was the word I used with my daughter—and God always pulled Mom through. This time, though, God was pulling Mom through the thin veil.

The Chicago-based band played loud, used foul language (something that I no longer cared for), and put on a good show. My daughter made her way in the crowd up close to the stage, and I was right behind her. Something about losing someone close makes you even more protective of the ones you have, and I felt a magnified protectiveness come over me as these people I didn't know stood and milled around us. I made noise when my daughter did and the more I made noise, the more fun my kid seemed to have and that was what the night was all about. I was helping my daughter have a good time, and I wouldn't trade the experience for anything in the world. Sometimes, I felt my heart drift to Mom, and tears escaped my eyes when I didn't want them to, but this my daughter didn't see. It was her night, and sadness couldn't be a part of it.

The drummer beat his drums so the waves of percussions could be felt on my chest. He twirled his sticks in the air, a feat I am sure he practiced, and without warning, he threw them straight at us. All the hands in the crowd in front of us reached high to grasp the drummer's sticks. The drumsticks bounced off fingertips like a beach ball. It had the same effect on my daughter's fingers as on all the other fingers when one of the drummer's sticks sailed over her fingertips—and then the stick fell to the ground between her and me. I grabbed the wooden stick and held it close to my chest and paused, not wanting to fight over it with our fellow concert lovers. I waited for all the frantic eyes to quit looking for the stick—and then I tapped my little girl on her shoulder. When she turned around, I held the coveted drumstick up between our faces, asking, "You want this?"

Her eyes almost outsized her face. She screamed and jumped up at least a foot in the air, and then, in a single motion, she grabbed a tight hold on the drummer's stick and hugged me with an excitement that every daddy wants to see in his child. This moment lasted only seconds, but I will hold onto and retain it in my heart for life—a true gift.

The band thundered, and everyone had fun. The drummer beat up his drums, the guitarists twisted their strings, and the singers did their best to stretch their mouths to the size of Mick Jagger's, and somehow, the music was great. But as with all things, good or bad, this concert came to an end, and the bright lights used for the dirt-track car racing came on. I followed my daughter and Juan to a little Mexican restaurant that stayed open for the late-night crowds. My daughter's company was much better than the food, but that was no slight to the food—it was just nice to be with her. My daughter is wonderful and beautiful, but then, parents who don't think so of their children suck as a father or mother. I held up my end of the conversation, but I was happy when I lay my head down on my daughter's living room floor, although I had sad, unconnected thoughts of Mom. Mom always believed in me.

***

The next morning, when the sun was just peeking through the windows, my grandkids were full of fire and excitement. They screamed, "Grandpa! Grandpa!" and jumped up and down, while my foggy head tried to clear. Indeed, these three little ones always made me feel like a Beatle or Elvis Presley in the way they reacted to my being with them. I often bragged that my grandkids were my fan club.

The boys held up their pet lizards for me to see, and I admired them. "What kind of lizards are these?" I inquired.

"Grandpa, they are geckos," Brandon informed me, with a tone like I was stupid. Cody played the Guitar Hero game and made me wonder if he might be a musician someday. Alyssa amazed me with her interest in Jesus, and she busted one of her brothers.

"Grandpa, Brandon says he doesn't believe in God," she said.

"Well, sweetheart, you need to be the example for him. Besides, I think your brother is just trying to be difficult," I told her. "You know how he likes to pick fights with you."

"Yeah," Alyssa agreed. But then she frowned and said, "Grandpa, some of the other kids at school says there isn't a God and that Jesus isn't real."

"Sweetheart, I think you shouldn't argue with them but just pray for them." This was the best wisdom that I had for this situation.

It was like she remembered that she had prayer at hand, and Alyssa smiled. "Okay, Grandpa, I can do that."

I was playing with the boys when I suddenly realized that their sister wasn't around. My daughter was busy making breakfast, and I asked her, "Where's Alyssa?" She motioned to the kitchen's pantry. When I opened the door to the pantry, I found Alyssa sitting cross-legged on the small chest freezer that was in there. It was her little hideaway, something that children sometimes find cozy, but maybe that was her time with Jesus. I believe that, more often than we know, it is when we are just relaxing that the Holy Spirit talks with our spirit and speaks into our hearts.

I didn't want to leave my daughter and grandchildren, but I had an hour's drive back to Mom's place. I was aiming to be there by the noon meal which seemed crazy because I didn't know what I was driving to. I didn't come to watch Mom die; I came to celebrate and honor her. Nothing made any sense, but I pressed on.

***

When I walked into the assisted living building, my brothers, sisters, and a few in-laws were there. Some were in the room with Mom, and some were in the living room-type area. These facilities have such areas to make the people who leave their loved ones there think it is like home but with friends their loved one's own age. There was always someone to visit our mother every day and to make sure that she was okay, but not all the folks there were so blessed.

I was numb with exhaustion. The knowledge of Mom's condition couldn't be absorbed in any part of my being, and I didn't want to think about it. It was like pouring oil into water; it wouldn't mix. It was good to see family, but everyone looked too sad. It was a pizza party to celebrate Mom's ninety-one years of life and the wonderfulness of our Mom being our Mom. I would have chosen Mom to be my mom if God had given me a choice. Mom taught us so much in life, mostly by her life and how she lived, which seemed so mundane and normal at the time, but when we understood, it stood out significantly. All of us were and are better for her patient example.

After a tornado destroyed her apartment in the same small town, she looked over what had been salvaged from the wreckage, as it lay helter-skelter around Sis's living room, and said, "I can either laugh or cry. I think I'll laugh." Then she sat quietly in deep thought for a moment. I believed then, as I do now, that she was reflecting on all the other tragedies she had known.

Mom was born in western Kansas in 1919 and lived through many disasters that effected the farmers of the area yet she always has a positive outlook on all situations. On a visit to Mom's home with my daughter and grandkids, when she was about eighty-five, Mom struggled with her walker, with the split tennis balls slipped over the walker's "feet," as she moved across her apartment's living room to get ice cream bars for my grandkids. My youngest grandson, Cody, sat with his mother and siblings in a row on Mom's sofa, all in perfect behavior. He asked, as if he was trying to comprehend oldness, "Grandma, are you old?"

I was the only one who had the vantage point to see Mom's face when he asked this question. A smile shot across her face, and her eyes twinkled with laughter lines, and she slowly turned around to face her interviewer. When Mom could fully see Cody's eyes, she said, "Yes, son, but some are older." Mom always found the positive and the angle that most people didn't see.

When I was a child, a new family moved into our part of the county. After a farm auction one spring, there was a discussion about this family among the farm folks, as they stood under elm trees on mowed grass. These auctions were a community affair; almost everyone was present. Even this new family was there, but they hung closely together. They were polite but didn't socialize very much. The group of men and women excluded this family from the discussion about them. The biggest part of this chat was about how poor they must be, judged by their patched clothes.

My mother only had listened up until this point—she hardly ever spoke her mind—so when she broke in with determination in her voice, everyone listened to her, "Their clothes may be old and worn, but they are clean. Now, they take care of what they have."

The group agreed and decided that they must be hard-working, honest folks. They did well after that.

At the assisted living unit, my family and I gathered at a table large enough for all of us. Romano's pizza was set in the middle on the neatly laid tablecloth, along with paper plates, red plastic Solo cups, pitchers of water, and large bottles of several kinds of sodas. We all settled down to eat—without Mom. Our oldest brother, whose hair had turned from brown to gray, sat at the head of the table. My older sister asked the eldest to give the blessing, and he did. His blessing was short, but how does one bless a birthday meal when the honored one is lying in bed, still breathing but without movement. How is this to be understood? How is such a day celebrated?

We did eat pizza and drink some sodas, and at some point, I placed my left hand on my eldest brother's shoulder and said to my captive audience, "Remember when our brother, here, was getting ready for his senior high school prom? His four-door '55 Chevy was parked in the driveway, shining like it had just come off the Chevrolet dealer's showroom floor, while he was in the bathroom in a black suit, combing his ducktail. We youngest three boys all kneeled down in the kitchen, watching him through the open bathroom door as he sang 'Mrs. Brown You've Got a Lovely Daughter'[3] and 'Oh, where, oh where can my baby be?'[4]"

This was like priming a water siphon because from there came a bunch of "remember when" stories. It was good to see some smiles and hear my

---

[3]   Written by Trevor Peacock, performed by Herman's Hermits, 1965.

[4]   "Last Kiss," written by James Lafayette Tarver.

family's stories—I couldn't bear the sadness. The family's chuckles were infectious but they were stilled when a cake was brought out.

Mom's birthday cake was beautiful. We all just looked at it, and one of my siblings said, "Let's all go in and tell Mom happy birthday."

My older sister held the white frosted and colorfully decorated cake as we all walked into Mom's room together. Mom was in the same position as she had been all day. I stood by the window, and Sis, with the cake in hand, stood at the foot of Mom's bed. She said in a loud voice, "Mom, it's your ninety-first birthday!"

Mom almost sat up in her bed. She opened her eyes for only a second, and she looked happy when she lay back down. Mom had made another goal and even this one was important. I believe it was important to God to help her reach her goals, even in the smallest detail, and to place it in her heart to request a pizza party for her last birthday, so her children would be with her to see her off. This occurred, while at the same moment, she looked through the thin veil to the people she had lost in the past—those she loved so much were on the other side, greeting her. On both ends of the journey, there was love. God is like that; He gives true gifts.

Mom was a goal-setter, and she had made it a goal to live to ninety-one. When she was sixty, she said, "I will live ten more years." When Mom turned seventy, she said, "I will live to be eighty years." When Mom was approaching eighty-five years she said, "I will live to see ninety." And again, by the time we had her ninetieth birthday party in a large room at the local hospital—she was already there after another spell—she said, "I will live one more year."

As Mom's ninetieth year pressed by, day by day, Sis and I discussed many times that Mom hadn't set another longevity goal. In the last months, when Sis would ask, "How are you?" Mom would answer, "How would you like it if you couldn't get out of bed?" Mom's bodily pain had become unbearable for her, and she didn't want the narcotic drugs needed to take the pain away. I think that God lets us suffer at the end of life so that we will want to go to heaven because who would want to leave the family and friends around them if it were pleasant to be here on the earthly side?

The afternoon was sad, but one has to remember that we were all so sad because Mom was a wonderful mom who had endured much. Mom was always a good mom and a lady toward neighbors and community. Money was often very short as we grew up, but Mom always had Kool-Aid for us kids. She made apple pies and apple crisp for us in the summer months, when our apple trees were giving their harvest. Mom did chores with us, and we learned old folk songs because she sang them in a soprano voice that only got sweeter with her age, and we kids joined in. She let us boys come in the house and watch afternoon cartoons when Dad was on the tractor in the fields, when we were supposed to be working on something in the barnyard, but she would rush us out as soon as Bugs Bunny and the others were over.

A couple of years earlier, when I'd taken my daughter and grandkids to see Mom, we agreed that we would all sit quiet while each one of us had a turn to sit in a chair next to Mom and talk with her individually. Sis had told me that Mom was in a lot of pain but that we should go ahead and spend some time with her. I led everyone down the corridor to Mom's apartment, and when we entered, I saw Mom's pained expression and that she was hunched over in her easy chair. Yet when Mom realized we were in the room, she sat up straight and smiled like she felt perfectly okay and it was a zip-a-dee-doo-dah day.

We all took our turns speaking with Mom, and she focused on us and our lives. When she talked with one of her great-grandsons, as he sat with his video game in his hands, she asked, "What do you have there?" He explained to Great-Grandma how it worked, and Mom asked good questions. Mom knew that these were special moments to be lived. She knew this time wouldn't happen again, and I am sure that my young grandson thought that Great-Grandma was ready to buy her own video game because she seemed so interested, but it was his well-being that Mom was interested in.

***

I had planned on sleeping at my big sister's house on Saturday night, but then, I had a plan of drinking beer with my brothers and sisters on that night. While we were together as a family that evening our gathering was actually a changing of the guard. I didn't think about it until much later, but even though I regularly walked in to check on Mom that night, I never pulled "guard duty." My siblings knew that I was worn out without my saying anything, and they let me sleep. I lay on the couch in the living room. I was chilly, but I didn't want to leave. In my dozing, I vaguely remember someone covering me with a blanket and pushing a pillow under my head while I dozed fretfully. My restless dreams were of Mom—just Mom.

When I awoke on the bright sunny Sunday morning, Mom was still with us, at least in breath. I went in Mom's room and waited. I looked at Mom. I spoke to Mom. And I waited. There was no response. The morning was in a dense haze, without movement of time. I wasn't ready to accept Mom's leaving me—leaving us. All my life, Mom was there—a constant, a trust, a love, a comfort. She was always at a hand's reach or at the end of a phone line or cellular signal. It was an impossible thought to think Mom could die. I just couldn't wrap my brain around the idea; the idea wouldn't even come near my heart. Mom was stability.

***

My plane was flying out early on Sunday afternoon, and there was two hours of driving time to get there; another hour was needed to jump through the TSA and ticket hoops, just to be treated like cattle once we were boarding the jet. I had the responsibility of going to the job site; it was waiting for my return and direction. Mom had taught me and all of us to work and the joy of work. Not working felt wrong; working felt right.

I said good-bye to everyone and, lastly, to Mom. I drove, numb and full of terror. Mom could not die. Mom had to recover. On the plane, I put my headphones on my head, and soft jazz filled my ears from my iPod. The plane finally bounced down on the heavy concrete at the airport, where my truck sat in a rented parking place. I drove to the job site, the Walmart remodel that was still in progress. I held the title to the travel trailer that I stayed in while working, but it was Mom's and would always be Mom's. Mom loved to travel, and this was the trailer that she and Dad had used. The little trailer was full of memories. Even a set of Mom's earrings hung on the curtains above the dining table, where she put them many years earlier when she was still bounding up and down the steps. I couldn't move her earrings—I guess it was in hopes that she would come walking in and put them on her ears, with a smile, with dark hair mixed in with her gray that now dominated her head. I could just see her admiring her jewelry in the full length mirror that hangs on the bathroom door.

I was walking down the back hallway of the store, surrounded by men who were asking me questions and taking my direction, when my cell phone rang. It was my eldest brother, and he said, "Mom is gone." His voice crackled when he said he had to go. He said that he loved me, and then he was gone. My head was battered with the thought. *Why didn't I stay and put off the flight for one more day?* Then, somehow, I found peace.

***

My daughter-in-law, Amanda, said that she wanted to go to Mom's funeral, and so after flying in from our respective locations, we met at the airport. My son—her husband—couldn't be there, as he is a Marine and at the time was in active duty on an aircraft carrier, somewhere in the Pacific Ocean. I was grateful, however, for Amanda's company. She made the funeral process a lot easier for me.

I was so exhausted that while I waited for her at the small Wichita airport, I fell asleep in one of those uncomfortable airport row chairs that can only be successfully used when sitting straight up. I must have been snoring loudly because when I woke up suddenly, I felt the stares of several people. One lady stared at me from a shop on the opposite side of the wide aisle. With everyone looking at me, I felt like I had unintentionally farted loudly in church. I felt I had no choice other than moving to another part of the airport so everyone would relax. I moved closer to the fenced-in area, where all the arriving passengers would come through, and it wasn't long before my son's sweet wife was there, with her cautious, caring smile. How I loved that smile. I had been struggling with the Walmart job; the men were not happy with me, and the job was behind schedule. A friendly face was exactly what I needed.

The drive to the small town where Mom's funeral was to be held was a blur for me. I had called ahead to reserve rooms at the only motel in town. We were blessed that it wasn't hunting season, when hunters from the surrounding cities flocked in to take out some of the pheasant, quail, or deer from the area—good for the local economy but little else. Charming and quaint would describe this town at first glance. On this Main Street was the movie theater where I saw my first movie, a British-made horror film called *Trog*.

I saw the movie with the children of Mom and Dad's friends, while our parents played ten-point pitch at their house on the northeast corner of town. Card playing was a pastime in this country area. Mom and Dad played a lot of card games with friends or at local card parties, held in the shutdown one-room schoolhouses that dotted the countryside.

The pastor of the United Brethren Church, later known as the United Methodist Church, baptized my mother in the North Solomon River when she was thirteen. We never doubted what would happen to Mom when she left this world. Mom had a solid faith. Mom took that step of faith in her baptism and is a part of the body of Christ that resides in heaven. Her faith—a path she never tired of traveling but relished and was displayed without intent on her part—showed in her daily actions and compassion. Those who knew Mom knew that all they had to do to see her in the afterlife was to work out their own salvation.

I slept hard in the not-too-comfortable motel bed and arose like I had a to-do list for the day. Sometimes, a person has to just get through things, knowing that friends and family were going to be around. In these situations, one just has to have a "stiff upper lip," as the British used to say. As a child, when someone who was important to my parents passed away, I wondered why they seemed unemotional. It looked as if they didn't care, but now I knew that it was something to be endured and that their insides were molten lava, pressuring their body's confines, trying to get out, but the person's personal strength kept the emotion constrained, least a crack occur and result in a complete meltdown. Now, I knew. Now, I comprehended what I wished to never learn.

Mom's funeral was at a Christian church on the corner of State Highway and Main Street, in the town where Dad and Mom retired.

It also was the county seat, where Dad and Mom farmed for twenty-two years. During Mom's funeral, my oldest brother's son strummed his acoustic guitar at the front of the church. Mom loved to sing Christian hymns, and in honor of her, we sang. I believe she is singing before the throne in heaven. She loved the song "In the Garden,"[5] and I can still hear her voice as she sang perfectly in tune, with eyes that seemed to look beyond with a contented face. When Mom was around eighty years of age, I stood next to her one Sunday in my childhood church, and I stopped singing for a moment so I could listen to her voice—it was always sweet and only got sweeter as the years traveled by. I remember that moment like I have a recording of it, and I play that DVD in my mind every day.

Everyone who could be at the funeral was there. Even ex-wives, distant family, and friends I had forgotten in my many years away showed up to say good-bye to Mom. I saw people from the different communities where Mom had lived—people that she would have a compliment for, whether it was the shirt they wore, how healthy they looked, their smile, or pointing out their kindness; Mom saw the worth in everyone, and many lives touched were honoring her this day.

I drove to the cemetery after the funeral with June Carter's words singing in my head: "Mr. Undertaker, please drive slow for this lady you are carrying; I hate to see her go."[6] I thought about Mom being in that hearse; I thought about all the other hearses I had followed down this same lonely road and that the Cadillac with Aunt Millie had slid around in the mud. As I watched its rear end swing back and forth and sling mud with its rear tires, I had worried, as a preteen, that she would be bounced back and forth in the back of that hearse.

I may have felt alone, but I wasn't. We all drove out to the little United Methodist church on the north side of a narrow sand road. Black evergreen trees lined the border around the church between the field and the buffalo-grass churchyard. The black evergreen trees also dotted the cemetery in various scraggly shapes, and where they just happened

---

5   Written by: C. Austin Miles in 1912.

6   "Will the Circle Be Unbroken," a Christian song written by Ada R. Habershon, with music by Charles H. Gabriel.

to grow, some of the trees had pushed tall gravestones over to an angle. The churchyard was cut out of a field and the graveyard cut out of a cattle pasture. The field around the church was often planted with wheat. It had lured us as kids, when the wheat was tall and golden. We were too small to understand the value of not injuring the wheat stalks while the heads filled with their fruit.

I was very familiar with the cemetery and knew most of the stone markers. I knew who was buried there, some personally and some by relation to someone else. I was at some of the funerals and knew older grave markers from years of moving and clipping grass by hand before Memorial Day and Labor Day each summer, as a member of the local 4-H Club—this is one way we earned money as a group for our activities. Whatever the memory attached, all around me was familiar.

Mom's grave was dug, the vault was in its place at the bottom of the pit, and chairs and canopy were all in order. The spot where Mom was to be laid to rest was next to Dad's resting place. Some other family was already laid in this row to the south. A wire fence on the west side of the cemetery was all that separated a farmer's cattle from the stone markers. A red white-faced cow calmly grazed just across the wire fence, as if nothing was happening; other cattle foraged close by. I don't think any of the farmers or country folks at this funeral even took notice of them. Cattle were such a common aspect of this life. I thought of Mom, many years earlier, milking cows in a long dress, with the tin pail held tightly between her knees as she sat on a one-legged stool.

The driver of the hearse most likely had driven my other family members to this same corner of the cemetery, and he knew where he needed to drive, even though there were no marked roads. He parked close to the last property Mom would own. Six of her oldest grandchildren carried her to the grave. Choosing the oldest to carry Mom was the only way to choose because as Mom said, "All my grandchildren are my favorite one." This love Mom had was for all, no matter how they came in the family. One had to even put up with a divorced spouse forever because Mom said, "Once a member of our family, always a member of our family." She loved her family. Mom just loved, simply loved.

Two of the six chosen to carry Mom were my son and my younger brother's son, but they both were serving military duty, of which we were proud, so my daughter and my nephew's stepbrother did the honor in their siblings' stead. Once Mom was placed on the stand above her grave, the preacher took his place and stood before us. Mom's body lay in the coffin in a soft lavender suit. Mom chose her suit and made sure that my older sister knew what she wanted. Dad had, in his love, bought Mom an expensive lavender suit, just like this suit, and Mom loved it, but she said that it was too expensive to go to the grave. She wanted someone to wear it. My oldest brother's wife proudly wore this lavender suit, and I'm sure she cannot wear it without thinking of her mother-in-law, who treated her like a daughter.

The country preacher said some words of encouragement, consultation, and teaching, to those who were actually listening. I know he had a tough job and did his best, but my mind pondered the fact that the body I looked at didn't appear to be Mom. Sure, it was Mom's body, but she didn't seem to be in it. And that is the hope—that one day we all receive a true gift, the gift of heaven. My family and I, as well as many old friends, watched as Mom was lowered in her vault to be stored away. Mom had made the request that we see her into the ground and placed in the vault, and we honored her request, even though we knew that if we hadn't, she wouldn't have scolded us for disobedience, as she did earlier in life. By this time we knew how valuable a mother we had, and we just did our best. A large bouquet of red roses lay on Mom's coffin, and because we knew that Mom was not a wasteful person, someone took off the bouquet right before the coffin descended. The flowers, symbolizing love, were handed out to the girls and women. My daughter-in-law, my daughter, and my granddaughter received their roses from my hand. Then the clicking of the lowering mechanism began. I am not sure why I stood close to watch her actually be placed in the bottom of the vault, but I did. Maybe it was just to make sure everything was right. Camron, one of Mom's great grandsons, not being much older than a toddler, also stood close by Mom's open grave, probably with more childhood curiosity than anything, yet we all knew how he loved his great-grandmother, and she loved him. When this boy came to visit her, he would play Mom's animated stuffed animals. When each animal was switched on, it would dance, twirl around or appear to be singing. Mom would laugh with pleasure when Camron—or Samuel or any other of the little ones—would do the "Chicken Dance"[7] with a stuffed chicken that she had. As the little ones danced in front of her recliner, she instructed, "Now turn around, now shake it, now put your arms like this and flap your wings." She instructed with humor in her eyes and her gentle way, and she and the child would laugh. Mom taught us that a joke was only a joke when all were laughing.

Now, Camron watched as the machine clicked and the straps lowered Mom to her last bodily destination. He leaned over a little more as the machine clicked, and then a little more, until some watchful person grabbed him so he wouldn't tumble in after Mom. He still was allowed to watch and ponder this happening. Mom would have chuckled to see Camron, in his curiosity, and I chose to believe she was chuckling from a better vantage point than we had.

---

[7]   A song composed by Werner Thomas in the 1950s.

29

Jesus, Tell Me,
"Go and Sin No More"

Jesus, may I touch Your holy robe?
Savior, mud my eyes so I can see.
Lord, drive my accusers away.
Jesus tell me, "Go and sin no more."

Holy One, how I need your healing.
Oh, with my tears, let me wash Your feet.
With what I have, let me serve You well.
By my Father's Word, shall I ever live.

God, give me this day my daily bread,
That in following You, I may live.
And when my house is all in order,
Fill me up with Your faithful glory.

Turn over the tables of the wicked.
Your glory is my guide and rear guard.
Lord, watch over my coming and going.
I enter Your gates with thanksgiving.

Jesus, tell me, "Go and sin no more."
Lord, drive my accusers away.
Savior, mud my eyes so I can see.
Jesus, may I touch Your holy robe?

— ❦ 30 ❦ —

An American Conversation

The truck driver was waiting to have his semi-truck repaired. The truck stop wasn't far from Mexican border at the southern tip of Texas, and South Padre Island was about an hour east. I was working at this truck stop, where I had a brief conversation with a truck-driving man. This particular day was cloud-covered, with high heat and humidity. I would guess the temperature was around 108 or so, with the humidity at a level that made one often think about taking a cool shower. The truck driver was dressed in shorts and a T-shirt, like most truckers these days, and he carried himself with self-confidence. My conversation with this trucker was about the heat and humidity. I realized that he was uncomfortable and not used to such weather, so I asked him where he was from.

He looked at me in a puzzled and concerned way, with a personal shield that had just gone up, and asked, "You mean original country or now?"

Sadness swept through me for a small second, thinking what this man must have been through in his life in order to instantly be so defensive. I said, "Now," and he smiled and responded, "Fort Worth!"

Then, after a congenial conversation about the differences in the weather from north to south Texas, especially in the Lower Rio Grande valley, we said "See you later" to each other, knowing we most likely would never see each other again. I gave him a nod of my head, and he gave me a slight bow.

﹡ 31 ﹡

Javier's Palm Tree

Javier stood on his parent's lawn where his mother had once stood. His mother had pointed to the spot where this forty-foot palm tree towered. He was silent and only looked unhappily at the tree. His younger brother admired the palm tree in its beauty, and he talked about how their father had made Javier keep the dead palm leaves trimmed. "Dead palm leaves hanging down are nests for rats, and have to be trimmed off," Their father had explained.

Javier had been required to water the tree and do everything to take care of it. His parents would never let his brother or two sisters help in any way with this palm tree, even though all other chores were taken care of as a family unit. Javier's mother would stay on his tail about this tree, like it was the most important tree on the property. The family's land had other trees—ash and oceanfront oaks that were bent by the sea breeze—which father and sons trimmed as a family chore every spring. The branches were burned, and the boy's sisters brought cool water out during the heat of the day. The great oaks were beautiful with their gnarly bent trunks and branches that struck out sideways, pointing to the inland, and then leafing out fully, creating the desired shade.

But this tree had some kind of significance. Javier's younger brother mentioned, "It was odd how Mom made you—and no one else—take care of this tree, and you did a good job, it lived a long time and is still growing."

Javier frowned. "And she made me plant it outside my bedroom window, so I had to look at it every day."

"Mom did, didn't she," his brother responded, realizing its location was odd and not lined up with anything else in the yard, "That's something I never thought about before."

"Why do you keep talking about that damn tree?" Javier turned and walked back into the house.

***

Thirty years earlier

Javier and his friend fell out of the battered truck he was driving. They both were laughing hard, and even when they began to walk toward the house, they kept bumping into or supporting each other. Lights came on in the house, and Javier's father stepped out onto the front porch, pushing his hair back. "You boys okay?"

"Oh we're great," Javier said through his laughter.

Javier's father gazed at his truck. "Where did you get that palm tree that's in the back of your pickup?"

"We found it."

This father glared at his son. "Set in a pot? You stole the tree." Just then, Javier's mother came out the screen door and without looking at her, Javier's father said, "Tell your mom what you've done."

"We found a palm tree, Mom." Javier wasn't giggling now; his eyes showed concern.

"It looks like it came from a nursery, and they were already closed by time you boys went out," she said. She walked out into the yard and pointed to where the tree was to grow. "Plant it right there."

"Okay, let me get some sleep, and I will get it planted tomorrow," Javier said.

"No, *mi 'jo*, you will dig the hole right now and plant it." His mom was firm.

"Hey, partner," Javier said, turning to his immobile friend, "get a shovel out of the shed in the backyard, and I will get the tree."

Javier's father became animated and pointed down the street. "Francisco, you go straight home, and don't delay. I am calling your father right now."

Francisco turned and almost ran home.

Javier dug the hole until his mother was satisfied that it was just right for the tree. He carried the tree over from the bed of his truck, and under his mother's instruction, he got out the knife that he always had in the glove box of his truck and cut the burlap off. Then, once his mother was satisfied that the tree's roots were raveled out enough, he placed the tree in its hole. Sweat poured off his head, and he looked sick in the hot South Texas night. His embroidered shirt was soaked, but his mother wouldn't let him cool himself when she made him get a five-gallon bucket to fill with water and pour in the hole around the tree roots. He just wanted to lie in his bed, but he followed his mother's instruction about packing the soil in around the tree just right. She stood there and instructed that the swale around the tree needed to be able to hold water, and then she had Javier fill the swale full of water. By the time the work was finished to his mother's specifications, the sun was coming up hot, and fatigue filled Javier's mind and body.

It was Sunday morning, and the family never missed Mass as a family unit. "*Mi 'jo*, get cleaned up for church, and I will have some breakfast made," his mother said. The family sat down for a light breakfast, but Javier wanted sleep and ate little. During church, if he let his eyes close just a little, he felt his mother push her elbow in his side. After church, when his father stopped the car in the front drive, his mother said, "That's a fine place for that tree. There is something special about that palm." Javier's father looked at his wife in bewilderment, as he had throughout the tree-planting process but didn't say a word.

After this, no instructions were given to Javier, so he went to his room to get some sleep. He sat on the edge of his bed to pull off his shoes, and his eyes fell on the palm tree that he had labored to plant, right outside his bedroom window.

Javier slept all afternoon, and when he rose up and walked out, his Mom looked right past her younger children and said, "Javier, go water your tree. You will water it every morning and evening." After that, it was known as "Javier's Tree," and as it grew, his father made him keep it trimmed, even when it required terrifying Javier on a tall extension ladder. Javier trembled as he climbed the ladder and wrapped an arm around the tree's truck to saw off dead palm leaves, while sweat dripped off his forehead.

***

The tree grew mightily and was still growing on the day his mother passed away, comfortably, in her own bed at home, after a long life. His younger brother looked at Javier's back as he walked to the house, and their father stepped up next to the younger brother with watery eyes and said, "Your mother was a wise woman. I don't believe Javier ever stole anything again."

─── ❦ 32 ❧ ───

Turtles and Bunnies

Our lawn was still wet with early morning dew. My older sister handed me an empty, cleaned cottage-cheese container with a construction paper handle looped over the top, forming a basket of sorts. She instructed me to choose the tender shoots of green grass from our front yard to fill the small basket I held in my hands. I thought it was a fun game but was bewildered as to who this Easter Bunny was that she talked about and why he would lay candy eggs on only the softest, greenest grass while we attended church.

We never ever gathered eggs from our rabbit cages, only from the henhouse, but I was assured that the Easter Bunny was a special bunny and not like the ones we kept in cages. When I questioned this idea of a bunny laying eggs, I received vague answers that didn't make sense to me. That was the tough part of being a toddler, as I heard that I was called. I was supposed to accept being told the strangest and most unlikely things—like a fat man in a red suit coming down a chimney when it was too cold to be outside, and he would do this in the dark. Not only did that not have any reason to it, but we didn't have a fireplace; we had a wood stove. Our woodstove had no latch on the inside of its cast-iron door, so anyone on the inside of the blazing-hot woodstove would not be able to get out and into our house. That's when I learned that there was this thing called magic, which seemed to be that answer for anything there wasn't an answer for.

I pondered these explanations while my hands grew wet and cold from the grass covered with last night's dew. My big sister knew a lot of things and was extremely wise, and my preschool hands did the best they could. Still, I required more guidance from Sis on how to find better bedding for the candy eggs, which was another problem. Eggs are supposed to be for cooking or hatching babies, and these were chocolate? It hadn't been that long ago that wise older sister explained that the little ducklings following the mama duck had come from the eggs she had in her nest, which I did see; these things were a lot easier to learn.

The whole ordeal came to an end when Mom called for us kids to come in to get dressed for church. Of course, I understood leaving for church much better when Sis explained that the Easter Bunny would only come if we were at church (whoever this weird bunny was). Then, after inspecting her younger siblings' baskets, Sis decided all our small bunny nests were adequate and gave us leave to go in. I was glad; I wanted to warm my red, wet hands.

The cottage-cheese container baskets were neatly arranged in the middle of our big dining room table, forcing me to ask how a bunny would get in the house and also be able to jump up on the table. Big sis once again gave me some of her unending knowledge and explained that the Easter Bunny was a magical bunny, giving him special abilities to accomplish such task. "Oh!" I said. There was that thought about magic being the answer again, whenever there was no other answer.

Dad didn't go to church with us on that morning. He said he had chores to do. I wondered if his presence would keep away this magical bunny. I had to find out about these eggs and if they would cause me to be magical when I ate them. It seemed strange to have Mom drive the Oldsmobile instead of Dad.

The lady who taught Sunday school told me that magic didn't exist. This was something to think about; maybe there just wasn't any magic in her life. After Sunday school and church services were completed, we headed home. I wondered at the excited anticipation of my older siblings for returning home for Easter Bunny eggs. I thought there must be something to it, and I was looking forward to arriving at home to find out what all the fuss was about.

The sun was warm and glowing when we pulled up to our farmhouse. Dad was walking up from the creek to the house to join us as we tumbled from the car. Mom parked it under the budding mulberry tree, which never had any berries on it, but they still called it a mulberry tree. When I asked if this was a magic mulberry tree, since it was able to hold the title without having any mulberries, I was told, "You ask too many questions."

I followed the hurrying troops ahead of me as fast as I could. These front porch steps were always an obstacle for me, making me slower. By the time I arrived in the house, everyone was oohing and ahhing over the Easter bounty. And that was interesting, but I wanted to take another look at the wonderful creature called a turtle.

My older brother had caught it somehow and put it in a big cardboard box in the dining room. I had to skirt all around the commotion to get to the box, which was between the bathroom door and my big brother's bedroom's door. This turtle was really interesting. It would try to snap at my fingers, and sometimes it hid inside a magnificent shell with lots of colors and bumps. It was the strangest animal I had ever seen in my couple of years—but where did it go! The cardboard box was empty!

The missing turtle was a big concern. With its not being in the box, it was most likely hiding in the house somewhere. Big brother had told me the turtle could bite my toes or fingers off in just one quick snap. The heck with that stupid rabbit and what he might have left us; we had a situation at hand. Somewhere in the house was a sneaky turtle, waiting to jump out and bite off toes or fingers.

I was trying unsuccessfully to get someone's attention to make the declaration that a dangerous creature was stalking our home when Dad stepped in the room. I went to him with all my staggering speed and grabbed his biggest finger with my fist to lead him to the empty turtle box. I explained the best I could in my small vocabulary, with many hand gestures and big eyes that we had a severe safety issue at hand. Once Dad understood, he stated with confidence that the turtle must not have liked living in the box and had gone to live in the creek.

This really confused me—a magic bunny that could open doors, get up on top of high tables to lay chocolate eggs on green grass in bowls, and safely reverse that trip; a turtle that had not been able to get out of a box for days suddenly escaped the box, opened the door to get out of the house, and made it to live happily in the creek.

God's creatures are amazing.

seanlovedale@outlook.com

Like my Facebook page.